SONIC
FROG
PRESS
- PRESENTS -

FROGMAN

MIDDLE SCHOOL'S MOST WANTED

BY E.R. COSENTINO

First Printing 2019
ISBN: 978-1-949562-90-3
Library of Congress Control Number:

Cover Images: Purchased and Licensed from www.99Designs.com
Cover Design: Phil Poole

FROGMAN

Middle School's Most Wanted

For Gia, Luca, Rocco

Many thanks to my sisters, Christie and Wendy; to my father, Don; and especially to my husband, Gino. I appreciate your love and support. Thanks to my editor, Ellen Dryer, as well as my illustrator, Phil Poole, for his amazing cover art. Thank you, Cassandra Smith, for pulling it all together. You all rock! All glory to our Heavenly Father!

Chapter One

I know what you're thinking. Believe me, it would sound crazy to me too, except I, Alex Addison, sixth-grader, know it's true. I can't deny I eat flies, have new webbed toes, and can seriously jump; like over houses. Last night was my scariest Halloween ever! Begging for candy door to door turned into a fiery rescue mission! I have one nasty splinter in my heel and a half burned-off eyebrow to prove it. Thank goodness for leftover Halloween makeup. But my new reality is this...after a chance encounter this past Labor Day weekend with a weird frog on the beach that peed on me, and weeks of spontaneous amphibian development, I became Frogman. There's only two people on the planet that know my secret identity; my little brother Sam and my best friend Artie.

Saturday, November 1st, the morning after saving Dirk the Jerk, sixth grade's biggest bully, and Piper Patterson, the coolest girl in sixth grade, from an accidental inferno of flames that could have melted the moon if it were made of cheese, I did what any kid would do. I ate pancakes. Sure, my mom's dream to make the historic Marshall House a state landmark had burned to the ground. Yes, the house actually burned down last night. Yes, she was crying into her cup of organic coffee while my four-year-old brother, Sam, made "ribbit" sounds as he nibbled his pancake into the shape of a frog. But what could I do? I acted natural and hid my shock at what was all over the front page of our town's newspaper, The Cedarville Gazette. My father, Eric Addison, held it up to show me how one of my best friends, Joel Hutchins, had made the paper again.

"Wow. This is incredible," my dad pointed to a collage of photographs of a blurry quadruped on the front page. "Maybe Joel is onto something. Maybe there really is an unusual creature in our community, an animal yet to be identified by science. But this doesn't look at all like Bigfoot. It says here in the article that Joel has named it, "Frogman.""

I tried to swallow, but pancake was stuck in my throat. If only it were Bigfoot. Joel has been obsessed with that creature, but now he has turned all of his attention towards Frogman, (which is ME).

"Have some orange juice." Dad poured me a glass, but my mother, Ellen a retired E.R. nurse turned organic seed-seller on the internet, was already standing over me ready to administer the Heimlich maneuver.

Yep, that's right. The slightest sniffle and my mom lines up Vitamin C tablets and fresh garlic that she demand I chew and swallow immediately. She is a champion in her cause to keep us healthy, and no donut hole or fun-size candy bar is too small to go unnoticed; except on Halloween. That's the day when we can feast on sugar and our pancreas can work overtime. If you're wondering... the pancakes are made from buckwheat and quinoa. Yeah, I know....

Though the photographs of "the creature" were dark and out of focus, I knew they were of me. Sam knew too, but as my parents had yet to recognize me, I tried to do what any normal kid would do who wasn't Frogman. I ate another pancake and tried to console my mom.

"Maybe it's a good thing the Marshall House burned down. Think of all the money the Historical Society will save. Think of all the time you would have spent fund raising to fix that old farm house. Now you have time to spend with your family and make pancakes."

Sam burped and Libby, my eighth-grade sister who thinks she's the boss of my life, blew a bubble with her gum then quickly turned and popped it.

7

Mom looked at us and tried to give her best, fake smile. She stirred her coffee and clinked her spoon hard against the side of her cup. She grimaced as she avoided the third call that morning on her cell phone from Debby Fisk, the Historical Society's volunteer Publicist. Mom took a quick sip and turned to Dad, "I can't possibly deal with this nightmare until I've finished my first cup. I'll call her back soon. I guess we'll be going out there this morning to assess the damages, but from the looks of Joel's photos it's a lost cause."

Dad hugged Mom and offered her his last piece of turkey bacon. Mom was chewing away when the front doorbell started buzzing as if someone was leaning against it. We sat there stunned into frozen silence. I thought for a moment that the police had come to arrest me. Could I go to jail for impersonating an amphibian while jumping out of a burning building with fellow classmates? Did they recognize me in the blurry photographs on the front page of the paper? Since I seemed to be the only one able to move, while my family just stared at each other in quiet wonderment, I answered the door. There on our front porch stood Artie Brandt, my best friend and tallest kid in our grade, and he was white as a marshmallow in a blizzard. He was holding the paper in both hands, and speaking so quietly that I could barely hear him. In between loud gulps of air I could hear the words, "If Joel... knows, life over, mad scientists will forever study you...doomed."

Chapter Two

I knew what Artie said was true. Joel Hutchins, my other best friend, who is also the second shortest kid in sixth grade, (I am the third shortest kid), is trying to create a career for himself searching for undiscovered animals, mostly Bigfoot. But now, Artie and I believe he has ditched all previous plans and has set his sights on Frogman. I invited Artie inside and gave him a look that meant, "Keep it together." Artie joined us at the kitchen table.

"What has you up so early this morning?" My dad asked without the slightest hint of suspicion. My mother was a different story altogether. "Artie, you look a bit pale and you're sweating. Do you have a fever?" Mom was feeling Artie's forehead with the back of her hand before he could sit down.

"No, not a fever, just real clammy. What did you do? Run all the way over here?"

Mom was back in her chair stirring her coffee again.

"Well, I came over to show Alex that Joel made the paper again. I see you already know that."

"Yes, I tell you, if he doesn't make it as a world class biologist, he should consider a career in publicity and marketing. That kid knows how to get press," Dad chuckled.

I didn't feel like laughing at all. I felt like I might vomit pancake all over my empty plate. Artie put the Gazette down in front of me and pointed to the incriminating photographs. Sam smiled real big, full of pride for me, his older brother, then said, "That was fun."

Mom's radar is always on, even when she sleeps, so nothing much ever gets by her. Now her internal alarm was going off and I could see panic and anger wash over her face like clouds roiling in a storm.

"Sam, where did the boys take you trick-or-treating last night? Which neighbors did you see?"

I began to answer for Sam but Mom quickly shushed me.

"No, I am asking Sam. Where did you boys go last night?"

Sam, mouth full of pancake and slobbery syrup, answered as truthfully as he could. "We went everywhere. It was awesome!"

"Did you go to the Marshall house? Were you there at the party?"

Sam looked at me and then at Artie and back to me. Mom was fuming. She looked me dead in the eye, "Please tell me that you were not at that party last night and that you are not responsible for burning down that wonderful house!"

Now Dad had put down his paper and was staring at me with interest.

"We did go trick-or treating, but we were not invited to the party, right Artie?" I tried to act calm.

"Right, we aren't part of the cool kid's club so we weren't invited." Artie answered in a tone that was slow and deliberate which only elevated my mom's suspicion. She leaned across the kitchen table and drilled holes through my eyeballs with her unflinching gaze. I blinked and decided I had to give her something.

"We were trick-or-treating on Westhaven Drive when we heard commotion coming from the direction of the Marshall House. We went to check out the noise. When we saw that the house was on fire, we stayed back from the house watching the fire trucks, police cars and ambulances."

"It was so awesome." Sam attacked another bite of pancake.

"I had no idea Joel was even there." I was telling the truth. I really had no idea Joel was going to be anywhere around that place, much less show up with a camera as I rescued Dirk and Piper from that fiery stack of sticks.

"I can't believe you took your baby brother to a fire! What were you thinking?"

"I didn't know there was going to be a fire! We just heard this noise and went to check it out. Sam was never in any danger. I promise, Mom." And that part was true. Sam was never in any danger. I made sure Artie kept Sam away from the fire.

"Right, Sam?"

Sam nodded his head in agreement and gurgled a mouthful of orange juice. The phone rang again. It was Debby Fisk. "I better answer this. It's her fourth call." Mom took the phone in the kitchen, spoke with hushed tones, and held her forehead with her hand." I knew it was bad. She hung up the phone and grabbed her purse.

"I am going to meet the ladies at the site to take stock of the situation. I'll be back soon. Artie, you are welcome to stay but in light of last night's adventures Alex now has to rake the leaves and turn over the compost bin. Then clean the bathrooms, toilets too. And you are grounded from all video games until you are 42 years old. That's right, 42! And you can never leave the house again. Ever. Except for school. I can't believe you ran headlong into a fire!"

Of course, my mom was exaggerating about that last bit for effect as she snatched up her car keys and went out the garage door. But her last statement was closer to the truth. I had to save them. I had no choice.

Chapter Three

Mom was gone three seconds when the phone rang again. "Did you see the Gazette, did you?!" It was Joel. He was shouting with excitement. "It's so awesome! I knew there was something fishy out there and now I have proof. Real proof: photographic evidence!!! People will have to start taking me seriously! My dad has already bought twenty copies of today's paper and the phone has not stopped ringing this morning! It's so crazy!!! Well, gotta run! See you later!!!" Then he hung up the phone. Artie's cell phone rang moments later and it was Mandy, Piper's friend, giving Artie an update about what happened last night since we were one of the few people left when the police, ambulances and fire trucks arrived.

After Artie got off the phone with Mandy, I put my breakfast dishes in the sink and we went to my room. Artie looked up and down the hallway to make sure no one had followed us then quickly closed my door. He turned to me and in a deadly, serious voice he said, "Alex, you got to lay low. Real low. Everyone is talking about this, and Joel has put every single picture he took last night up on his Facelook page. His page got so much traffic it's stopped working. This is bad; REAL bad."

I slumped on my bed scared. All I could think about was how hard it is to get through middle school, to be accepted and liked. If everyone knew that I ate worms and have webbed toes that look like some weird foot disease, the school would probably create a special classroom just for me. I would sit alone all day long so that I couldn't give anyone warts.

"I think your days of saving the world are over, unless of course, you want Joel to dissect you like a dead frog. Oh, sorry," Artie cringed at his choice of words.

"But… The only thing is, I am Frogman. I'm glad I was able to save Piper and Dirk the jerk. I like jumping over houses. I like sticking to stuff. I even like flies."

"Speaking of flies…Dirk already accused you of eating flies in the cafeteria and let's not forget you are the one who ate his boogers for Fear Factor Friday. No more gross or froggy behavior. I think if you want to continue to help people when they really need it, you need to lay low until this blows over."

"You're right, "I sighed. "No more stunts. No more taking crazy chances. Joel is smarter than I thought."

After I finished my chores and shot baskets with Artie, I logged onto Joel's Facelook page. It was much worse than what Artie had told me. Joel had really good pictures of me. Still, you'd have a hard time telling it was me, since I was covered in a thick coat of slimy mud. But that night on the ten o'clock news my nightmare began to unfold. Joel was the lead story on television. They interviewed him at the site of the burned down house as he relived the rescue by Cedarville's newest cryptid and possible superhero. "It was huge. It was muddy and super froggy. It's obviously an unknown superhero! I have uploaded my pictures on all my social media sites. Don't forget to like and follow me on pages."

Our local news reporter, Kelly Meadows, turned to our Police Chief Bob Carlton, who quickly dismissed Joel's comments. "We are confident that there is a normal and unsurprising explanation for events surrounding the Marshall House fire." He then urged the public to come forward with any information about this incident. The Chief ended the interview by reciting the toll free number to their Tipster Hotline, assuring all calls would be confidential.

Great, I thought. The local police are investigating me. I went to bed wondering if I should just turn myself in. But I didn't do anything wrong. What good could come from it if I confessed that I was Frogman? Would they try to blame me for the fire?

Artie had been right all along. Frogman would have to disappear for a while until everyone lost interest.

Chapter Four

The next morning was Sunday, so we ate breakfast and ran off to church. Normally church is a place where we eat donuts, play a crazy game and then have Bible study; but not this morning. Nate, our new youth leader, was bombarded by new and sudden interest in current events. Clearly, he was the only person in town who had not seen or read the news the day before. He was baffled by all the questions regarding Frogman.

"Was Frogman hanging out with Adam and Eve in the Garden of Paradise?"

"Was Frogman on the Ark with Noah?"

"Can Frogman swim?"

"Is Frogman good or evil?"

"Does Frogman go to church?"

Nate rubbed his chin, "Well what you're telling me is that this Frogman saved Piper Patterson and Dirk Crawley from a fiery inferno. He risked his life to save them so I think Frogman must be somewhat good. That's quite a heroic act. Since I don't know who Frogman is and have never met him, it's hard to determine if he goes to church or not. But if he is a living and breathing creature then he was created, right? He didn't come from nowhere. Something doesn't come from nothing, right? That's one of the first laws of physics. We all were created. Was he on the ark, well, I would have to guess that if it lives on land and breathes air then it's forefather had to be on that boat or it wouldn't be here. That's all I got on Frogman for now, so let's start on today's lesson."

Even though I was glad that Nate thinks that Frogman must be somewhat heroic, I was not prepared for this debate. I threw up my donut twice in my mouth while my identity was being discussed.

Sunday afternoon I tried to pretend to be happy for Joel. He had taped his interview on the news from the night before and uploaded it onto his Facelook page. As of 4:00 p.m. on Sunday, he had received over 60,000 hits. Every two hours he would call to give me an update on the number of people checking out his Facelook page. He was so pumped up by all the attention I feared he would forget about Bigfoot and commit the rest of his life to the study of Frogman, which is ME!

His last phone call to me Sunday night was minutes before ten p.m. He called to tell me that two Sheriff's deputies had dropped by to check out his pictures. They plugged his camera into their laptop and uploaded his SD card. He made sure his mother captured the moment with her cellphone. My throat tightened and I squeezed out, "Super." Even though I could barely speak above a whisper and now felt like I was being strangled by Bigfoot himself, Joel didn't notice my gasps for air and stifled moans of despair. He continued on, "This is just so awesome. You know that the CIA and our military have the technology to use satellites in outer space to hone in on a golf ball and read the name of the company that's printed on it. Just think what they might be able to find out using spy technology with these photos. I just wish the house had burned down during the day."

"   What?" I strained to suck in more air. "Why would you have wanted that old house to burn down?"

"No, I meant, I wish there was more light. Since it was already dark, it's hard to see Frogman's details. I wish it could have been a daytime sighting. I could know more about this creature. But the good news is, these deputies will be able to enhance the photos in ways I could only dream of."

I went to bed in a cold sweat and lay awake wondering what I was going to do tomorrow. Everyone would be talking about this. Everyone. Once Joel posted his photographs with higher resolution I would become the big weirdo. My life would be dogmeat.

The next morning at school was chaotic. No one could settle down to think about multiplying fractions or misplacing modifiers. Joel was basking in the glory of his triumphant coup of the local media. Students lined up with notebooks, text books, and copies of the local paper. Joel happily signed them all. He also auto-graphed arms, hands and tennis shoes. Even Principal Evans asked for his signature as he unfolded the front page of the Cedarville Gazette.

In every class, teachers asked for a retelling of last Friday night's events, and Joel, not wanting to disappoint, happily gave a play-by-play of that evening's activities followed up by a dramatic read-ing of the front page article of the Gazette. He kept them eating out of his hand by promising more revelations at the proper time. I was happy for Joel, in a way, since everyone has given him a hard time about his obsession with Bigfoot since kindergarten. No one was making fun of him. He was finally being taken seriously. But now, I had to find out what this new revelation was before it was released to the public. I had to stop Joel in his tracks.

Dirk, on the other hand, was questioned in each class too, but you could clearly see he wanted to forget about Friday night. He gave one-word answers and stated that he didn't remember being rescued. He suggested he must have had too much smoke inhalation. All he really remembered was trying to save Piper. Everyone would have to wait for Piper's side of the story because she wasn't at school. She was at home recovering from the traumatic event. Mandy, one of Piper's best friends, gave her side of the story and agreed that Joel was telling the truth.

Trying to fit in and trying not to panic with all the new interest in Frogman, I made a few comments to create doubt within Mandy's story. "Geesh, it was so hot, I had to stand back really far from that fire. With all of the smoke, it was hard to see anything." Only two students agreed with me. I had no control over this story and where it was heading.

School was such a disorganized mess that day, that no one noticed, teachers included, that there was a new student. CJ Dillon had the unfortunate luck to begin school on the first Monday after the fiery Halloween. I think he was in just as much shock as I was as to how much time was spent on last Friday's events rather than focusing on social studies. Our teacher didn't flinch when a reporter showed up outside the school requesting an interview with Joel. As soon as Joel left the classroom, everyone jumped up and ran to the window to watch the impromptu meeting. When Joel returned, the teacher asked Joel to give his account of the interview in front of the whole class. Joel spent the next thirty minutes describing his four-minute conversation with the reporter. That evening, Joel's story and photos had spread beyond our community in the Texas hill country. Joel was on the six o'clock news in Houston and Dallas.

Tuesday morning rolled around. I brushed my teeth and prayed that today would return to normal. I hoped that teachers would remember to teach and that everyone would forget about Frogman. But Tuesday didn't turn out like I expected. Here's what happened:

Mr. Johnston watched the clock on the back wall, as students trailed in and found their desks. He fumbled with a piece of paper several times and drew circles on the page with a red pen. When the bell rang, he walked over to the door, shut it and returned to his desk as he eyed each and every one of us. He turned around and grabbed up the paper off of his desk and began that day's class.

"Class, I have a special announcement. We have a new student to welcome this morning. CJ Dillon, would you please come forward and tell us about yourself." Mr. Johnston coughed slightly into his hand then scanned the room for our new classmate. It was at this point I realized that Mr. Johnston still had no clue what our names were or who we were. I guess teaching sixth grade for 24 years will do that to you. From the back row, a tan, blonde, and somewhat tall boy rose from his seat and walked to the front of the room. He turned around to face us and these were his exact words...

"I'm CJ Dillon, though that's not my real name, still you can call me CJ. I've just moved here from up north but I'm not really supposed to talk about it or I could be putting your life in danger. That's really all you need to know about me. Oh, I can say that I like to play football, basketball, and baseball." Everyone watched as he slowly walked back to his desk and took his seat again. Even Mr. Johnston was staring. After what seemed like several minutes of quiet whispers, more staring, and the soft ticking of the clock, Mr. Johnston finally pulled it together and directed us to section three of our text book.

By the beginning of fourth period every sixth grader knew of CJ Dillon. I was so happy Joel was bumped off the sixth-grade news ticker and CJ was now headline news. I know Joel was bummed about losing his newly found fame at school, especially to some new kid. I should have felt some sympathy for him, but I was excited to see Piper back at school.

Piper had come back to school with a nasty bruise on her forehead and a bandage on her arm. She was getting plenty of attention from her gang of friends, the Glitterati, a group of girls who have no fear of glitter, sequins and rhinestones. It is their love of their favorite color "Shiny" that binds them as friends. The Glitterati met with her after each class at her locker. They spoke in hushed tones and bedazzled her bandage and after fourth period tried to disguise her bruised forehead with make-up. It didn't work. Still, she was the coolest and prettiest girl in sixth grade. Unfortunately, CJ had seen her too.

I guess you could say CJ is a good-looking guy. He's taller than Todd Highfield, our sixth grade super athlete. Yeah, he has broad shoulders and some muscles, but don't we all have muscles? I mean everyone has muscles or how else could we smile or frown? I guess I must have been frowning because Artie kept asking me what was wrong all through lunch. I didn't want to talk about it. Piper couldn't stop staring at CJ.

By Wednesday, November 5, rumors and bets were flying across campus about CJ's mysterious background, and why he could put everyone in danger if he said too much. Here is the list of the top five rumors in order:

1. CJ was a witness to a heinous crime and is in the witness protection program. Obviously, the bad guys are still trying to find him.

2. He is a secret agent working for a new child spy program instituted by the C.I.A. and his case is so closely guarded that only the President knows his real name.

3.   He is in a boy band from England and is trying to finish up his sixth grade year without interference from adoring fan girls. Fortunately, he'll be leaving soon to go back on tour this summer.

4.   He just landed his own reality television show.

5.   He is a complete and total nutter.

I guess you know where I placed my bet on that list. Whether CJ was just another delusional sixth-grader made no difference to me, as long as Joel was no longer the talk of the sixth grade, our community, or on the front page of our local paper. I crossed my fingers and hoped that Joel and everyone else would forget about Frogman.

Chapter Five

With CJ Dillon making headline news all over school, Joel consoled himself with feeding the class snake in Mr. Jameson's Science Class. Even though Fluffy, a small orange striped corn snake, had been living in Mr. Jameson's classroom for two years, I had become horribly afraid of these reptiles since becoming Frogman. After all, snakes eat frogs.

Fluffy spent her days curled up in a back corner of her aquarium except when Joel dropped by with an offering of a dead mouse or crickets. Earlier that morning, Mr. Jameson had taken a dead, frozen mouse out of the classroom freezer and left it on the counter to thaw. (I have to say, I was a bit curious to know what that icy treat tasted like.) Joel, under Mr. Jameson's instructions, was to be discreet about feeding Fluffy her breakfast since there were more than several squeamish girls in the sixth grade. Joel stood at the back of the class while several boys stood around to watch. With all the boys watching fluffy, the "ooooh's" and "ahhhh's" had begun, but then one of the boys moved from the front of the aquarium and gave a full view of Fluffy enjoying her breakfast.

Shrieks and screams filled the classroom and Mr. Jameson clapped his hands and shouted for the classroom to calm down. Everyone quieted after a few more seconds, except me. I was standing in the doorway, wild-eyed, panting. I saw too much. In that brief second of fluffy eating breakfast, I had a horrible vision of being eaten by a snake. I had to get out of there and collect myself. I was excused to the bathroom and when I came back moments later, our seats had been rearranged. Apparently, Lance didn't like sitting near Fluffy, as well as a few other students. Now Piper was sitting diagonally across from CJ Dillon. That was way too close. Mr. Jameson began his lesson on layers of the earth while I calmed myself watching Gertie, the classroom guinea pig, spin her exercise wheel.

After school, I sat in my bedroom reading. After all, I am grounded from video games for another 10, 946 days. That's when Artie dropped by. He looked fine but for the layer of sweat that coated his face and arms. I feared the worst and was almost too afraid to ask what had happened. Unlike myself, I knew Artie was not afraid of snakes.

"Alex, you have to help. You must. I can't do it without you. Besides my mom already called your mom and it's really a done deal. I think I'm going to throw up."

"Of course, whatever you need. I'm there. Just tell me what's going on." My stomach turned with those last words. I didn't know what I was getting into and I had just promised him earlier to lay low.

Not only has my dad signed up to be one of our basketball coaches but now he has decided to run a basketball camp during Christmas break. It's just so awful. My life is ruined."

"Really? Your dad is going to run a basketball camp just for us?" I was trying hard not to explode with excitement.

"Sure, fine. It isn't the same for you. Go ahead and celebrate but he's not your father. You're not expected to walk in his ginormous, super-sized footsteps. I hate basketball! Why couldn't he have been a world class horse shoe pitching champion. Nobody cares if you decide not to throw horse shoes."

"Look, basketball starts next week and this is all going to be a good thing. You can't outrun this. Have you ever thought that maybe your dad decided to help coach and run this camp so he can spend more time with you? Remember he told you that he was an absolute klutz when he was your age. He knows you're terrible."

"Yeah, he does." Artie flopped onto my bed landing like a splayed-out octopus.

"See, he's just trying to help in his own way. Just like my dad tries to connect with me when he talks about how incredible Atari was and how I'm missing out on real video games. Pong...really?"

"Was your dad on the top-rated Sports Network playing Pong?"

"Ok, you got me. Still, we will get through this together. We don't have to be champions. We're just playing for fun."

There was a knock on my bedroom door and then a bark. Ranger, Joel's beagle pup, came running into my room followed by Joel. Ranger immediately smelled my sock-covered feet then ran back and forth in front of my closet door. Could he smell my winter stash of dead bugs hidden at the bottom of my closet? Did dogs care about bugs? Artie's left eye started to twitch.

"Hey guys! You want the good news or the bad news first?"

My stomach pitched as I worried that his good news had to do with exposing me as Frogman. "I guess the bad news, first..." I really didn't want to hear any more news about his search, but I had to play along as a very supportive friend.

"I intercepted another piece of intel this afternoon in English. Turns out that Piper thinks that new kid, CJ, that weirdo, who thinks he's a super spy, is... get this..." Joel pulled out a piece of paper from his back pocket and unfolded it. He quickly found his place in the note and read aloud. "O.k., it's right here somewhere, got it... He's sooooo cute. "So" is spelled with five "o's" by the way," Joel flashed the note around to show Artie and me that he wasn't exaggerating the "So" part of the letter. He continued to read aloud but now in a girly high-pitched voice, "He reminds me of Shane on that T.V. show that I love so much where everyone dances, sings, and they all work making snow cones on that Pier in San Diego." Joel shuddered, rolled his eyes and read some more, "You're sooooo right! CJ is soooooo cute! I wonder what his real name is?" Joel then pointed to the five hearts of various sizes drawn along the bottom edge of the note.

Joel hurled himself back then forward pretending to gag. He crumpled the letter and tossed it into the trash can. "Something must be done. He must be stopped. This has gotten way out of hand. Even Mandy has been taken in by his devious ways. There's no way that he's a spy or in a boy band. I doubt his real name is "Harry" too. I know hoaxes and this is a hoax." Joel paced the room.

I wanted to vomit. I had been so happy that Joel was no longer the talk of sixth grade and our community that I hadn't considered what it would be like to add another suitor for Piper's attention. I have known Piper since were in kindergarten. Even when she had to go to speech therapy in first and second grade, I knew she was special. She couldn't even say her name correctly but it didn't matter. She liked football, video games, and was always nice to the misfits in class. Even now, as a member of the Glitterati, she isn't stuck up. She is pretty and kind, which is why Dirk Crawley, aka Dirk the Jerk, is always trying to stake his claim to Piper while he and his goons, Kevin and Randy try to make me eat their boogers. Just as I was wrapping my brain around the thought that Piper liked CJ, Joel gave us the good news. Just like that; without any warning.

"The segment featuring me and the mysterious Frogman that ran on our local news last Saturday night is going to run tonight on GBN news. I'm going national!! National!!!! Joel was jumping around the room. Can you believe it? Set your DVR's for ten o'clock. I'm back on. I heard that they are re-editing it and it's going to be forty seconds longer. Forty whole seconds! I hope Mandy will be watching. I'm sure once she sees it she will forget about that stupid hoaxer CJ.

Chapter Six

    I sat with my parents watching GBN news at ten. Mom and Dad cheered as Joel's interview re-aired to a much larger audience. Instead of our small town of 3,000, a subdivision of a bigger city of 300,000 people. GBN news is watched by an estimated ten million people each and every broadcast, including tonight. I've heard that people even watch this news hour overseas. My stomach pitched as the GBN reporter asked Police Chief Carlton if he had any idea who the hero is. I gagged, then tried to smile when my father looked over at me giving me two thumbs up. With her eyes glued to the television, Mom leaned over to me and asked if I was sure I had not seen this thing that was in Joel's pictures. "Uhmmm, Mom, I think I would remember seeing that crazy costume."

    Then the camera cut back to Police Chief Carlton for more questions surrounding the strange person or creature seen in one of Joel's photographs.

"Can you add any new information in regards to the harrowing incident?" The correspondent asked while shoving the microphone under Police Chief Carlton's chin.

"We are following up on every lead and looking under every stone." Police Chief Carlton gave a reassuring smile.

"Is there any reason that the public should be concerned at this point? Joel Hutchins is pretty convincing that this was not a..."

"Let me go ahead and interrupt here." Police Chief Carlton cleared his throat, "We are still in the early stages of our investigation. We are meeting with many witnesses and asking the public's help for any information in regards to this case, please call us at our Tipster Hotline." The number flashed across the bottom of the television screen. "We are very grateful that no one was hurt in this incident. As always, be aware of your surroundings, and safety first."

As the camera closed in on a tight shot of the correspondent, she continued, "We received word earlier today from Cedarville's District Attorney that no charges will be filed. Again, I would like to stress that no one was seriously injured. Back to you."

Thursday morning before school, Artie and I stood by Joel's locker as Joel gave his "play by play" of last night's GBN Newsreel. That story had put him on the national stage as a budding biologist. I had watched it with my family, so I already knew what Joel was going to tell us. The interview did include more photographs that Joel had taken and more "airtime" with the local firemen who were there on sight. It was amazing to think that millions of people saw one of my best friends on television. But then the realization hit me that I had been seen by millions of people too.

"My dad checked the ratings this morning from last night's program. It was watched by nine million people. Nine whole million people! Can you believe it?" I don't think I have ever seen Joel so happy, then just as quick, he frowned, furrowing his brows. Mandy, Julie and Piper were huddled together in the hall, laughing as they passed around Julie's cell phone. "I wonder if Mandy saw me? I hope so, because if she did, she would see that what I am doing is real and that CJ is a stupid hoaxer."

At that exact moment, CJ walked up to the girls and greeted them. Julie quickly passed him her phone and he looked down at the screen, swiped it a few times with his finger and laughed with them as well. The four of them turned together down the hall and walked to class. Any anxious feelings that remained at the thought of my secret identity being investigated on a national news segment drained away. Joel, on the other hand, pounded his locker door with his fist, "I will prove to the whole world and the sixth grade that he is a faker! Anyone can see what a faker he is! Poor Mandy; She has been deceived. She is bewitched. I will save her!"

Artie and I rolled our eyes. Clearly Joel was back to watching, "Crown and Shield," the newest medieval show on television. Yeah, lots of knights and dragons. By the way, Joel likes dragons too. Joel's imaginary quest to take down CJ was cemented in his mind when eye witness accounts of CJ's throwing skills made the rounds during gym. Coach McGrath had us warm up by running two laps around the track at the beginning of class. This was no big deal except the class couldn't help but notice CJ, Dirk, and Todd Highfield out in front leading the pack. As we neared the finish line, CJ, Dirk, and Todd took off in an explosive burst of energy and the race was on to see who would finish first. CJ crossed the line a half second in front of Dirk, and two seconds before Todd.

Clearly, Dirk and Todd were trying to brush it off, but I could tell CJ had gotten under their skin. Dirk was muttering to himself on his way back to the center of the field. Kevin and Randy ran to his side, but Dirk wasn't having it. He stormed off to the other side of the field away from CJ. Todd seemed dazed as he walked in circles holding his sides and looking down at his feet. Coach McGrath blew his lucky whistle calling us to the center of the field.

We were then divided into two teams for a friendly game of flag football. It was also where we (the rest of us who are not on the Cedarville Lobos sixth grade league football team) realized we had missed an exciting night on the practice field only the evening before. Apparently, CJ has a really good arm. Once we started playing, we saw it for ourselves. CJ quarterbacked the team Joel and I were on, while Todd quarterbacked the team Artie was on. CJ out-threw Todd. After the first three touch down passes we were all in shock. Todd was disturbed and rattled. Dirk was angry. Real angry. He didn't like CJ threatening Todd's position as sixth grade's best quarterback. Joel was mad too. He kicked the grass on the sidelines doing his best impression of a serial sod killer. He was convinced that CJ was not twelve years old, but was indeed a community college drop-out.

Once we were back in the gym locker room and CJ and Todd changed clothes and left for class, the locker room erupted into a full-scale debate, complete with controversy. And here was the rub. Wednesday night on the practice field CJ told Coach Finley that he played quarterback and always had. Coach Finley informed him that Todd was their starting quarterback but he would consider him for second string. CJ wasn't happy at all, but threw passes to the team's wide receiver, hitting him on the numbers. CJ never missed. By now, the other coaches stopped their drills and every member on the team watched this wonder boy. After practice, Todd kicked his helmet across the field and stormed off to the locker room.

Coach Finley called him back in front of everyone, and lectured Todd about attitude issues. After giving Coach 50 push-ups, Todd grabbed his helmet and sulked off the field. The team was divided. Some want Todd as their quarterback and others said CJ should get a try.

Todd's day got worse too. In English, he lost his homework. The assignment was worth 20% of our grade. In Math, he got caught passing a note to his ever-faithful buddy and center, Josh Watterson. Rumor was the note was all about CJ. This of course was just more fuel to Joel's fire. "See what he is doing? He is tearing apart the team and all of sixth grade. I tell you, he's not eleven or twelve."

"You know you have to have a birth certificate to enroll in school, so I am pretty sure he's a kid like us." I tried to keep Joel from going all spider monkey on CJ. Did I like the fact that Piper and her friends were watching his every move across the cafeteria and that they were now Facelook friends...? No! Was there a whole lot I could do about it at this moment? Not really. Had CJ proved himself to be a child war lord, who was at this very second assembling nuclear missiles from an ice fortress in the Arctic Circle? I'm betting not. Still, Joel didn't like the looks of him. After a few moments, Joel agreed that he would give CJ another chance to prove he wasn't trying to make Joel's life miserable.

While walking to our next class, Artie and I were overcome by the delicious smell of cinnamon and baked bread. We followed this heavenly scent to the doorway of the Family Consumer Science class. Mrs. Mears stood over the open door of a stove at the front of the classroom. Several seventh grade students squeezed past us in the door way and walked to the back of the classroom to take their seats.

"Oh, good, GOLLY! WHAT in the WORLD? How did this happen?" Mrs. Mears reached further into the oven. From where we stood, it looked like she was climbing inside of it. "Come here, you little dickens! There you go!" Mrs. Mears took a muffin pan out of the oven and clanged it on top of the stove in front of her. She was shutting the oven door when she saw me and smiled. Waving her oven mitt through wisps of smoke, she asked, "Alex, are you in my class? We're having cinnamon rolls!"

I wanted one. I really did. But Mrs. Mears' hair was on FIRE!

"Do something..." Artie nudged me forward.

I looked around for anything that I could use to put out the fire. Near her was a pitcher of water, and next to that was a yellow ceramic mixing bowl. I couldn't jump to her because more students were pushing past us and taking their seats. They would definitely see me. Instead, I flicked my tongue to grab the water pitcher when a seventh grader bumped me from behind as she came into the classroom. My aim was thrown off course. My tongue stuck to that yellow bowl and I panicked. I PANICKED! I lifted that bowl and dumped it upside down on her head. Mrs. Mears screamed as icing glopped down her face and onto her blouse. She pulled the bowl off her head and with it her wig. Yep, Mrs. Mears' wig was smoldering at the bottom of the bowl of icing.

"What in the World? Today is not my day." She wiped the icing of her face and shirt, when she realized the bowl of icing was sending up smoke tendrils toward the ceiling. She glanced inside the bowl, screamed again, and grabbed a cup towel. Then, as if nothing was wrong, strange, or had ever been on fire, she tied a cup towel like a scarf over her head.

"Bye..." I gave a quick wave and bolted down the hall.

"What were you thinking? Those students might have seen you?" Alex poked me on the shoulder super hard.

"Are you kidding? You said, "do something." She was on fire. What choice did I have?" I replied. "I don't think anyone saw me. It was kinda hard not to look at Mrs. Mears without her wig on and covered in icing."

"Well...from now on, no more crazy heroics. No more stunts. It's too risky right now. Joel will definitely find you out, as well as the school, the police, and your mom, to name but a few."

"O.k., got it." But inside, I was already struggling with the new plan. Now that I am Frogman, how can I go around and pretend that I'm not?

"And, you should have gone for the water? I will never be able to eat another cinnamon roll again without thinking about her wig in all that awesome icing. It's so gross!" Artie covered his mouth to hold back a mini-vomit.

I agreed that icing with wig hairs is disgusting, but there was no time to talk. I had to get to my next class. Rushing through hallways, I couldn't help but think, How do I ignore people who need a little help? How do I ignore my funky frog feet, or my crazy new jumping skills? I will have to figure this out.

Joel was back on top by the time Mr. Jameson's class ended. After flopping his backpack onto his desk, Joel made a straight line to check on Fluffy and the temperature of the glass aquarium before class began. Students slowly entered the class unaware of the trouble that was brewing until Lance noticed that Joel had removed the lid off the aquarium and was now pulling out a small piece of branch, several larger rocks, and water dish.

"What are you doing? That snake is deadly. We'll all die!" Lance shivered, shuffling toward the classroom door. The students saw the panic on Lance's face and everyone, all at once, turned to the back of the class where Joel stood holding up a second small branch.

"Fluffy's not in here! She's gone." Joel put down the second branch and ran his fingers along the bottom of the aquarium, ignoring screams and shouts.

Mr. Jameson walked into the classroom to find Lance holding onto the doorjamb ready to make an extremely hasty exit, and three girls huddled together on top of his large metal desk, their shoes scuffing and wrinkling his papers.

"What is going on here? Get off my desk! Quiet, everyone! Stop Shouting!!" Mr. Jameson clapped his hands, but no one was listening. Especially Lance, who was now running through the hall to the nurse's office, yelling that he was allergic to snakes.

"I demand to know what is going on?!!" Mr. Jameson tried once more, as students stood on their desks or chairs.

From the back of the classroom, Joel yelled as loud as I have ever heard him. "STOP SCREAMING! YOU MUST STOP SCREAMING! YOU'RE MAKING IT WORSE!" The class quieted except for my deep, heavy breaths as I stood on my chair.

"Mr. Jameson, I am sorry to say that Fluffy got out. I don't know how... but she escaped! The lid was tightly placed on her aquarium."

Chapter Seven

"What?!" Mr. Jameson took long, quick strides to the back of the classroom. In seconds, he was standing next to Joel examining the aquarium with the deftness of a toddler with a plastic beach shovel. Pebbles and dirt hit the floor as Mr. Jameson shook and turned the aquarium on its side scooping out the bottom of Fluffy's glass condo.

Mr. Jameson whipped around to face us just as the bell rang signaling the official start of class. "Students, we are going to take a little detour today in our class itinerary and instead spend the next ten minutes looking for Fluffy. Ben, will you guard the door to make sure nothing goes in or out. The rest of you, please continue to stand on your chairs as we search the classroom. Fluffy must have found a hiding place to get away from the light and noise. Joel, check the corners. I will check the cabinets."

Mr. Jameson opened the cabinet doors just below Fluffy's aquarium. The classroom immediately broke out into, "Fluffy, here Fluffy. Come on girl. Here, Fluffy...." Mr. Jameson frantically searched the cabinets, drawers, and peered into the air vents. Joel took a different approach. He scanned the room, neither looking at the floor nor the ceiling. He surveyed the room as if looking at a crime scene. He just stood still. Then out of the corner of my eye I saw Julie, Piper's friend shudder, then, gasp. She trembled as she tried to speak but no words came forth. Joel, in an instant, was onto her. We both followed her eye-line to where she was gawking. It was Piper's backpack. I have to say, there isn't anything too out of the ordinary about it. It's blue with a supersized zipper pull made of rhinestones and blue beads. Blue is Piper's second favorite color next to glitter. She always dresses in colors that coordinate with her backpack: blue, mint green, and purple. I would know her backpack anywhere except there was a bit of orange escaping her outside pack pocket.

I seized up, my muscles paralyzed with panic and terror. After all, snakes eat frogs, but depending on the size of the snake, frogs will eat a snake. It is a hard truth to accept, I know, and ever since sixth grade started I have never dreamed of eating Fluffy. Actually, every day I try to forget that Fluffy exists. That's why I nabbed a seat near the front of the classroom. But at that moment, I tried to forget that I only ate a power bar at breakfast, because my stomach is growling. I started sweating, afraid I could lose control and gobble Fluffy right here in front of everyone. What is wrong with me? I am supposed to be laying low.

Now I imagined that Fluffy would taste like bacon. I really love bacon. Especially real, greasy, pork bacon, not the fake bacon my mom makes me eat. But before I could find out Fluffy's flavor, Joel stood between me and Piper, blocking my chance for a snakey snack. Joel clutched one strap of Piper's backpack as CJ clenched the other strap. Poor Fluffy retreated back into the pocket.

"Unhand this backpack, immediately!" Joel was not fooling around. His nostrils were flaring like a horse in battle. CJ smirked and towered over him. "Ummm, yeah... I don't think so. I think you need to let go so we can get Fluffy back to her stupid aquarium."

"Are you refusing to let go?"

"Yeah, I kinda am." CJ tightened his grip on the backpack.

"I will have you know that Fluffy is a rare specimen of snake."

"Isn't she an ordinary corn snake that is sold in pet stores across North America, including Mexico?" CJ kept his eyes on Joel, never looking down at the backpack. "Yeah, I thought so."

"Back away from the bag and back away from Fluffy," Joel demanded.

"I can't do that. I wouldn't want someone, like say, Piper here, to get a nasty little bite from Fluffy. Wouldn't that be awful? And the longer you hold onto this bag the more opportunity Piper has of getting a disease-filled bite on her arm or hand. You are now putting her at risk."

"Fluffy is a healthy, non-diseased snake. You're the one with the DISEASE!" Joel snorted a laugh."

CJ pulled back with all his might and yanked the backpack out of Joel's hands. The backpack flew through the air and landed on my desk. I know I'm supposed to lay low but what choice did I have? I righted the backpack on my desk, gently reached into the front pocket and pulled out a shaken corn snake. Fluffy immediately latched onto one of my fingers. Maybe she knew what I had been thinking, that I was hungry for a snack, or maybe she wondered if I tasted like frog. Either way the temptation was getting the better of me when I pulled her off my finger and then tried to smell her rich, baconey goodness.

"All right, all right. Let's get Fluffy back to her aquarium. I'm just glad no one was hurt or Fluffy, for that matter." Mr. Jameson quickly walked over and scooped Fluffy into his hand as she gratefully twisted around his arm. "Alex, have you been bit?"

"It's nothing. I think she was just afraid after CJ threw her across the room." I was backing up Joel here. CJ was completely unreasonable. Joel had it under control. Besides I don't want Piper to have any more reasons to like CJ than she already does.

"Why don't you go to the nurse's office and get that cleaned up. And while you're out, if you see Lance tell him it's safe to return to class." Mr. Jameson and Joel put Fluffy's aquarium back together and returned Fluffy to her heat lamp and log. There were no other escapes in class and Lance cautiously returned to his seat, looking over his shoulder back at the aquarium every few minutes until it was time for our next period."

After class as I stood at my locker spinning the combination lock, Piper walked up to me and said, "Thank you." She said it so quietly, I almost missed it. I just stood there dumbstruck. Then she walked away, joining Julie and Mandy in the hall. As the three of them turned a corner disappearing from view, she looked back at me and smiled. Maybe I wouldn't always be a booger-eater to her for the rest of my life. Maybe I wouldn't always be the sixth-grade football screw-up. I was so fired-up that Piper acknowledged my existence I wanted to jump and stick to something but I couldn't since I was being watched. CJ stood in the middle of the hall, staring at me. He didn't smile. He didn't frown. I felt cold looking back at him. Without a word, CJ turned and followed after Piper and her friends.

Seconds later Joel appeared with Artie to walk to our next class. "Hey, thanks for sticking up for me and letting Mr. Jameson know what a phony CJ is. By the way, are you feeling okay? For a second there you looked dazed and confused like you were going to eat Fluffy?"

Artie gave me a crazy-eyed look that screamed, "What?!"

"What?... No, way. I think I was surprised when she bit me. I didn't know she could clamp down so hard." I helped up my bandaged finger that had been smeared with antiseptic ointment. The nurse was on the phone with my mom for fifteen minutes, as my mom searched for corn snakes and their diseases on the internet at home. Once she was satisfied that my skin would not rot from the snake bite, was I allowed to return to class.

"Too bad it wasn't CJ that got bit. I wish Fluffy had chomped on his finger, but then we would have to rush her to a veterinarian for shots in case she caught a horrible epidemic from CJ. I bet he is full of gross viruses and germy bugs."

My stomach gurgled just hearing Joel mention the word, "bugs." I wished it was time for lunch. "Good thing Fluffy is no longer in danger. That's what counts." I really hoped I never wanted to eat Fluffy again.

"I don't think Fluffy is out of danger. Not as long as CJ remains at this school. There is no way she was able to just slip out of her aquarium. That lid was on tight! No, someone took her out and put her in Piper's backpack. I bet this someone is willing to put any innocent creature at risk to be a fake hero. We must defend all God's creatures against CJ's horribleness. Who's with me?!" Joel put out his hand forcing Artie and I to lay our hands on top of his, as if we were the Three Musketeers. If we had had swords, I'm positive he would have had us all clink them together and cheer, "One for all and all for one!" He really needs to stop watching "Crown and Shield." Joel went to class, but Artie hung back to talk to me.

"How is wanting to eat Fluffy laying low? You're supposed to be laying low."

"I rescued her from Piper's book bag. It wasn't a big deal."

"No book bag. No snakes. No fire. Lay low!" Artie was staring me down.

"Ok. Got it. I will stay away from fire and Fluffy."

"Good, let's get to class."

Chapter Eight

Now that we were into November, the PTA was in fundraising mode with their Christmas catalogs. Mom can't resist most magazines. She was drawing circles around wrapping paper she liked, as Libby flipped through another catalog full of popcorn and chocolate candy. It was at this point that Mom informed us that she had invited a family to dinner. It was her way of welcoming them to the neighborhood. Apparently, we were all going to a football game together.

"What? You don't even like football. You could barely watch me kick the ball for only a handful of games. How is it that we are all going to a game tonight?"

"It's the polite thing to do. I met a mother at the farmer's market today and she was just lovely. She's new to the area and I am going to help her get settled into our neighborhood. She can meet other mothers at the game tonight. Besides, her boys play. What's wrong with reaching out and making a new friend?"

I was completely in shock. Not that my mom was being nice and helpful. But that she was actually going to watch guys knock each other down, with great possibility of bodily pain and suffering. I, of course, was ecstatic! I called Artie and Joel to meet me at the game.

We ate an early dinner. Since Mom had just visited the farmer's market, that meant we would be eating a plateful of vegetables. Mom fired up the grill on the patio and Sam, Libby and I were instructed to run through the house and pick up misplaced shoes, backpacks, basketballs, and 1001 plastic linking blocks and put them away in their place. Libby wiped down the kitchen and dining room. I helped Sam wash his hands. He decided now was a good time to work on his finger paint masterpiece titled, "Killer robot fights Frogman."

"Nice work, little man, but we're supposed to be cleaning up, not dragging art supplies out into the living room. Mom invited some people over for dinner. We have to clean."

"Frogman has to clean? No, Frogman doesn't clean. Frogman gets the bad guys!"

"Shhhhhhh... Stop with the Frogman stuff, alright? That's between you and me. And right now, there are no bad guys here."

"Even Frogman's brother has to clean?"

"Yes, Frogman's brother has to clean."

I returned from the bathroom where I caught Sam pouring liquid hand soap all over the bathroom sink and floor when Dad came home. Within seconds, the "buzzing" of the front door bell interrupted our frantic sterilization and deodorizing of our house. Mom's new friend was early.

Mom introduced us to her new friend, Jackie and her daughter, Katie, a third grader at our elementary school. We sat down and quickly ate our dinner of roasted vegetables and tofu turkey patty. I know it is kinda gross, but you do get used to it after a while. Katie, on the other hand, looked as if she had never seen a vegetable and that at any second her carrots might attack her.

Her mother, Jackie, never noticed Katie was in fear of her dinner. She asked about my mom's internet business of selling heirloom seeds for gardening and about the pros and cons of raising your own milk goat. Libby finished off her last piece of asparagus and then snuck a piece of gum into her mouth. This swift move did not go unnoticed by Katie who was now pleading with her eyes for a piece of gum. Reluctantly, Libby reached into her pocket and slid the piece of gum over to Katie under her napkin. Katie perked up and unwrapped her gum out in the open. This drew my dad's attention away from his dinner. He frowned at Libby but didn't say a word. I think he figured that if Jackie didn't mind, why should he? He excused us from the table saying we would be leaving soon for the football field.

As I gathered up my plate and silverware from the table, my dad leaned across the table and asked me quietly if I was o.k. with going to the field. "You know, because you aren't on the team anymore." Dad seemed genuinely concerned.

"No, I'm completely o.k. with it. I just want to see the Cedarville Lobos beat the Anderson Armadillos."

"Got it. I was wondering if you needed a hug or not." Dad moved his fist toward mine and we fist pumped. "I'm glad we could talk it out."

Mom told us we would be leaving in fifteen minutes, and while we waited to leave she showed Jackie her compost pile and garden. Libby dashed to her room and locked the door and I got stuck with Katie. Great. I had babysitting duty. Standing in the kitchen, smacking her gum, Katie scowled at Sam and me.

Sam was never one to let any girl's foul temper discourage him. After all he had experience with Libby as his sister. He invited her into the other room to view his art exhibit. Standing over his depiction of Frogman, Katie smacked her gum.

"Yuck. What is that?" Katie frowned and then swallowed her gum.

"That's Frogman. He's a superhero." Sam was pointing at the painting, indicating the "super" part of a froggish looking man with a red cape standing atop a tall building.

"What does he do?" Katie tried to act interested by putting her finger on the froggish character.

"No. It's still wet." Sam hollered.

Katie looked at her finger and wiped the paint off onto her jeans.

"Frogman jumps and rescues people and sticks to stuff. He's awesome!"

"I've never heard of him. What's so great about sticking to stuff?" Katie shrugged.

"He's great! Right, Alex? He's great! You're Great!" Sam stammered folding his arms like Dad does when he's mad.

"Yes, I guess Frogman is great and so are you Sam, and Katie. Well, I can't wait to get to the game and watch some GREEEEAAAT Football! Who's with me?" I went to high-five Katie but thankfully she turned toward the backdoor to join her mom outside to look at dead leaves and banana peels in the compost pile.

"No Sam. Just. No. No more talking about Frogman. No one will understand. Got it?" I leaned over him. Sam started to cry.

"Ye...Ye...Yessss..." Sam grabbed my leg and rubbed his snot on my jeans.

Chapter Nine

Jackie and Katie followed us in their car to the football field while my family and I squished together in my dad's Honda. I was so excited to go, I didn't care that I was crammed against Sam and his booster seat. It wasn't very often that our family went anywhere where two teams battled over a ball. Mom's idea of a fun family outing is the Natural Science Museum where we can enjoy the inner workings of our bodies through plastic models and old sketches.

On the way to the game, Sam kept trying to whisper to me that I should have jumped on Katie's head.

"Sam, shhhh. You're talking too loudly. Besides it's not nice to jump on people."

"She doesn't believe."

"A lot of people won't understand. It's okay. She's only a third grader."

Mom turned back to look at us sitting in the backseat and gave us all a smile. "What are you talking about back there?"

"Nothing, just excited to see the game, right Sam?" I nudged him with my elbow.

"Yes." Sam was not very convincing as he frowned, staring out the window. "Do those people have to come with us?"

"Sam!" Mom was immediately riled. "That is not nice. They are new to our area and we are helping them to settle in. If we moved to a new neighborhood, wouldn't it be wonderful to have new friends show us around? So, be nice! That's an order!"

"Guys, your mom is right. Be on your best behavior. We are about to park and once we exit this vehicle it is all smiles, got it? Be helpful." Dad snapped his fingers and reached his hand into the back seat, trying to grab whatever knee, leg or foot that was in close proximity. Sam shrieked with giggles, but dad was not amused.

Mom, Dad and Jackie sat on the fifty-yard line, only five rows up off the field. Katie darted to the top of the stands and Mom sent the three of us to baby sit her. Once I was at the top I could see Artie and

Joel looking around for me. I waved and they came to join us. Joel brought Ranger, who was back to sniffing around my feet and barking incessantly. Libby rolled her eyes, gave Katie another piece of gum and deserted us by climbing back down the stands. She ditched us to sit alone on the bottom bench to read a book. Now Artie and Joel understood my predicament. They realized that I was not only watching Sam but had added a third-grader with an attitude to my list of responsibilities.

"So the only reason your mom let you come to a game was to babysit?"

"It's not so much babysitting as it is...well, yeah, I think I have been hijacked into watching her. My mom just met her mother and now they are all sitting down there with my dad. Typical."

"I have a bit of good news" Joel motioned for Artie and me to come in close so he could whisper. "Police Chief Carlton called my house when I got home from school. He asked again if I had any more pictures in case I had forgotten to give every last snap shot to those two police officers. He also let my mom know that two Texas Rangers were meeting with his staff. Isn't this exciting? Two Texas Rangers! But that's not the best part...."

I forced a smile and crossed and uncrossed my arms in front of my chest trying to hide anxious spasms that were surging from my stomach into my shoulders and neck. I was terrified to know what was coming next. I didn't want to hear anymore. I wished he was talking about two baseball players, but I knew he meant the finest lawmen in the whole state. And now these super cops were examining Joel's photographs. How could I keep my identity secret from the Texas Rangers?

"What's the best part?" Artie's left eye was twitching so hard and fast that he literally covered it with his hand. "Uhhh...I think I got something in my eye." Artie kept his hand over his eye as he looked from me to Joel and back to me again with one eyeball.

"Ya'll are being super weird," Joel scoffed. "Okay, after the phone call with Police Chief Carlton, the phone rang again. Ya'll will never believe this...I hardly believe it myself." Joel was grinning ear to ear. "Soren Bergman, America's foremost cryptozoologist called me!" Joel exuberance was shaking the aluminum benches we were sitting on. Several people below us turned around and gave us all the 'stink eye.' Joel tried to calm himself by sitting on his hands. "He's coming on Wednesday to interview me. My evidence is going to premiere on his show! This is what I have been waiting for. Vindication! He's coming to talk to me. ME!"

I was still a bit shaky but I had no idea what he was talking about. "Soren Who? Crypto-what?"

"It's only what I have been saying since kindergarten!" Joel was seriously frustrated with Artie and me. "Cryptozoology is the search for animals that have not been proven to exist!"

Sometimes it's hard to listen to your friend when they are talking about the boogey man being real. I mean when you're five, this is not news you want to hear. You also don't want to think about how doing your chores could lead to your sudden and untimely death. Joel has told me that people have had encounters with an upright, bipedal, hairy thing while taking out their trash at night. I still run outside to the trash cans like something horrible is chasing me whether it's dark or not. When I was in fourth grade, I screamed every time I saw the neighbor's cat creep past the mailbox at the end of my driveway. Joel's mood changed when we asked to hear about Soren, his favorite cryptozoologist. Soren, is the writer, producer, star of "Beast T.V." Apparently, he is a very big deal in the Crypto-world, but how would I know that?

So now I am being pursued by the Texas Rangers and a television host. At this point, I may be finishing up middle school through correspondence courses at a juvenile detention center or have my own reality television show. Or worse, a reality television show set at a juvenile detention center. I wanted to jump out of my skin, but I don't think that is possible.

The game was now underway as the clock ticked down the seconds in the first quarter but Katie had zero interest in a football game. Instead she was in a heated argument with Sam about superheros existing and how a frog would never make a good superhero. "They're slimy, squatty, green like broccoli, and they live in mud. Ewww! Who wants to get rescued by that? They could pee on you!"

"Actually, Sam is right." Joel couldn't resist joining the conversation. "There is something here that is unknown. We in the community have dubbed it, "Frogman." I'm certain that it is a favorable and quite possibly an honorable being."

"There's no such thing. There's no Santa Claus, Tooth Fairy, Easter Bunny or Unicorns. There's no such thing!" Katie crossed her arms and blew a bubble at Joel. She had no idea she had met her match, because Joel had never been one to back down.

"I never claimed that Santa Claus was real. I know there's no Easter Bunny. I am a man of science! There must be proof, positive evidence, repeatable results," Joel fired back at little 'Miss Priss.' He was so intent on winning the debate that it took him and the rest of us a few seconds to understand what happened, to hear Sam's wailing over the cheering crowd.

Sam gushed tears. Streams of snot ran down his chin. He attached himself to my leg. He didn't have to tell me what was wrong. I knew instantly. Katie had robbed him of his childhood. She had stolen fairytales, birthday wishes, and the illusion that a quarter can come out of your ear. Katie was evil.

I shushed Joel and gave him my best death-ray stare. Then I turned my attention to her, the little dark lord. "Katie, not cool. He's in pre-school and you're on your own."

I picked up Sam in my arms and walked down the stairs. "Sam, she's only in third grade. What do third-graders know. She doesn't believe that Frogman is real. You and I know he is, so don't worry about what she says." I couldn't deal with this awful little girl. What else might she do? Pick up Ranger by his ears and feed him to a pack of stray cats? I needed to distract Sam so I could calm him down and watch the game. Since we arrived, I had watched a total of three plays. Coated in Sam's slime, I decided a cup of hot chocolate would make him feel better. But first, I made a quick pit stop to grab a few dollars from Dad.

"What's wrong with Sam. Is he hurt?" Dad stood up to check Sam but was hip-checked by Mom.

Standing over me and Sam, she checked his teeth, ears, scalp, nose, arms and legs with the swift energy of a chimpanzee on twenty energy drinks. "No, no...I don't see anything? Honey, where do you hurt?" Sam was still wailing. "Hon, you need to use your words...where's your boo-boo?" Sam ignored my mom's pleas and buried his head into my shoulder.

I pulled Mom to the side and whispered into ear, "He's not hurt. Katie isn't used to little kids and told him there's no Santa. He just needs a hot chocolate. He'll forget about it in a little while."

Normally, Mom wouldn't be up for a dehydrated mix of modified milk products, sugar, and artificial flavors. She looked up at the top of the stands where Katie was standing against the back rail of the bleachers. Katie was smirking and twirling her hair.

"Okay, she leaned over and reached into her purse and pulled out a twenty dollar bill. Get a hot chocolate for everyone." She leaned over to Sam and stroked his hair, "It's going to be alright. How about some cocoa?"

Sam was happier after his second hot chocolate. We hung around the concession stand when out of the corner of my eye, I saw Katie waving her arms trying to get our attention. She pointed to the concession stand and pretended to drink from an invisible cup.

Joel and Artie noticed her too, and while clearly understanding her game of charades, they decided to egg her on. Joel kept scrunching up his shoulders and lifting his hands and mouthing the word over and over, "What? What?" Artie took a different approach to annoying Katie. He decided to cup his hand to his ear as if he was trying to hear her, then motioned to his wrist that he wasn't wearing a watch.

"Hey, I think we need another hot chocolate for Katie because if my mom finds out, I'll be in trouble," I said. Joel grabbed a five dollar bill from my hand and walked back to the concession stand.

I turned back in Katie's direction to find Katie dangling from the top rail of the bleachers. Whether she had tried to climb down the back of the bleachers, or somehow flipped over the rail by accident, she was about to fall. She swayed over twenty feet above the ground, holding on by one hand.

"Artie!" I yelled. Artie turned to see Katie and dropped his hot chocolate. "Run!" We sprinted towards the back of the bleachers. I wanted to jump. I knew I could reach her and grab her and land safely on the ground within two seconds, but I couldn't. My secret would be revealed. Too many people were milling around and clearly Katie was not to be trusted. Besides Joel was close by and I might as well show him my feet and prepare for seclusion in a secret lab away from family and friends. Either way, my life would be over.

As Artie and I reached the back of the bleachers I said a prayer, "God, what am I supposed to do now? How do I get her...?" Before I could finish my prayer, Katie's fingers slipped off the metal rail, sending sixty pounds of screaming human missile hurdling toward earth where Artie and I stood. The shrieking human rocket hit its target, (by target, I mean Artie and me) flattening us against the cold, hard ground. Looking up at the sky, I realized that God's plan obviously included me becoming a human bulls-eye. As I said a little "Thank you" to Him that I was still alive, I tried to remove Katie's shoe from in front of my face. She kicked my head as she sat up. Artie was splayed out cold. Katie, crying, seemed somewhat grateful when Joel walked up with a cup of hot chocolate. She snuffled a whimper and walked back around to the front of the bleachers to sit with her mother.

"Man, that was awesome! You guys fell out like a pancake. I wonder if Artie's breathing? Joel nudged Artie's shoulder with his shoe and Ranger licked his hand. It wasn't until Ranger covered Artie's cheek with a good dose of puppy slobber that Artie came to.

Wiping his face, he sat up and looked around. "What happened? Who drank my hot chocolate?" The bottom of his jeans and shoes were covered in spilled cocoa and now Ranger, as if he perfectly understood the English language, was licking the end of Artie's pant leg.

It was at this point that Mom, Dad, and Jackie ran to us with a reluctant Katie trailing behind sipping her cocoa. "Alex, Artie... are you alright? Can you move? No, don't move. That's an order!" Mom was in full-fledged triage mode as if she were starring in her own one-woman battle field movie. She tried to clear the area as best she could as more parents and kids were moving in close to see if we were alright. Apparently, Katie's fall was witnessed by more than just Joel. Even Piper's mom stood by us, asking my mom if she should call 911. Then the next thing I knew the paramedics that normally are on the sidelines of the football field were checking Artie and Katie's eyes with small flashlights and asking them what day it was and who was president. That's when Artie shook Ranger from his pants leg and stood up. "Oh, man... my drink went everywhere." Artie is hungry all the time and doesn't like to waste food, not even an instant hot chocolate.

The paramedics were satisfied that he was fine and then they turned to me. They checked my eyes and asked me if I knew where I was and which teams were playing against each other tonight. Then they asked me if anything hurt. That's when I knew I was in trouble, because I was pretty certain that Katie's elbow had ground into my ankle. My foot throbbed with pain but I couldn't tell them that, could I? They would want me to wiggle my foot around and probably have me remove my sock and shoe. Then in front of thirty bystanders, my parents, and Joel, I would have to explain the amazing webbing of skin between my toes that had not been there only a few months earlier.

"No, I'm pretty good. I have to say, I'm not hurting anywhere, at all, not one bit. I feel great." I smiled and stood up as best I could without wincing in pain. Pain shot up through my leg into my back from my right ankle, but still I put my full weight onto my right foot. I had to sell it so I kept on smiling. "Is Katie alright?" I wanted to deflect any and all eyes from me. "Thank you so much for catching her when she fell. I hate to think what could have happened." Jackie said giving Artie and me hugs.

Artie looked at me with a bit of a puzzled expression. Then Joel chimed in.

"Oh, no. It wasn't that they caught her," Joel said cheerfully. "It was more like they stood under her to break her fall. It was Awesome!! I saw the whole thing. They didn't stand a chance. Katie was barely holding on when they got to her."

Jackie's face turned pale. My mom's face turned ashen. Dad put his hand on Mom's shoulder. "The point is," Dad coughed, trying to remove the worry from his voice, "everyone is alright. No one's hurt. The boys broke her fall. They did succeed in keeping her from breaking any bones. I say we get back to the game, and you guys will sit with us, down front." Dad clapped his hands together signaling for us all to get in line and march to our seats. I sucked in my breath every time I stepped down on my right foot. Joel and Artie didn't seem to notice, but it was Mom I was worried about. If she had a super power it would be to sniff out bodily trauma.

We took our seats. As luck would have it, Mom was busy fawning over Katie. In return for our good deed, Katie gave all four of us lingering, angry scowls and sat with her mom who fed her chocolate candies out of her purse. I really don't think Jackie is into health food the way my mom assumes she is. Sam was still miffed at Katie and every time he got a chance, he stuck his tongue out at her.

The clock ticked down to half-time when I realized that Piper was trying to get my attention from the track. She walked away from the other cheerleaders and ran up to the stands right below where we were seated.

She yelled up at me, "You guys okay?" I, of course, looked around wondering who she was talking too. She laughed and pointed at me, motioning for me to come down to her. Joel and Artie were stunned by this show of recognition. Joel looked around to see if Mandy was watching. Mandy and a few of the Glitterati gang turned to watch as I walked down the few rows of bleachers to where Piper was waiting.

"Are you guys okay? I heard what happened. You saved a little girl from a terrible fall."

"Ummm..." I didn't know what to say. Piper was actually talking to me. "Yeah, well she looked like she was in trouble."

"Wow. Still, that was huge." Piper smiled at me and ran back to her squad who were lining up to jump around and scream. Though Piper still had her arm bandaged and decorated with rhinestones, she still held onto one pom-pom. Even with one pom-pom she is the best cheerleader ever.

When I got back to my seat, Joel was dying to know what she said.

"Did she ask about me? Did she say anything about Mandy asking about me? Don't look now, but Mandy is looking over here. Be cool, be cool." Joel then cuddled Ranger up to his face which brought Mandy and the Glitterati straight over to us. It was at this point that Artie reminded me again to lay low. But all I could think was, "How much lower could I go? I was splattered across the pavement like, well, froggy roadkill."

We spent the evening watching the girls pass Ranger around the stands and traded "evil eyes" with Katie. By the way, our team won, just not in a way anyone could have guessed. Todd threw a pass into the end zone for a touchdown. While everyone watched the ball spiral through the air and into the receiver's hands, one of the linemen from the other team had tackled Todd. We found out later that as the lineman was getting up off the ground, he kicked Todd in the hand and stepped on his arm. No one noticed this display of bad sportsmanship until Todd fought back. Todd jumped up and pushed the lineman down with a wrestler's takedown. All you could see after that was arms and legs tangled together. Todd is also on the wrestling team. The other team's lineman apparently is not. You could hear his yelps, whines, and cries for help across the field. The referees ran to the pair and Todd was escorted off the field and onto the bench. He was ejected from the game.

The night got worse for Todd. CJ was about to let everyone know he was this game's MVP. Sure, CJ threw passes, and marched our team down to the Armadillos end zone, but it was his running and diving that brought the crowd to their feet. CJ ran in four touchdowns.

Joel was now so annoyed by the very thought of CJ that he couldn't enjoy his third cup of hot chocolate. Mandy and the girls were even huddled together on the cold bleachers next to us as the temperature dropped. Mandy held Ranger and talked to Joel about dog breeds and the latest in doggy fashion now found on aisle nine at Poodle's Pet Salon and Spa. I could tell Joel was fuming with inner rage and wasn't listening to a word his "dear" Mandy was saying.

Without any dispute, he agreed that Ranger looked terrific wearing Julie's sparkly pink hair scrunchy around his neck. He also agreed that Ranger's dark green collar didn't coordinate well with Ranger's complexion. Joel was so blinded by anger he didn't notice that Ranger's nails had been painted light blue.

Chapter Ten

Friday was not a good day at school for Joel, Todd, Josh and even Dirk. CJ was the talk of the school again. The Glitterati were now CJ's biggest fans. I wasn't happy that Piper and CJ traded notes in class, but on the other hand, Joel had not mentioned "Frogman" in twelve hours. Joel had a horrible headache all day Friday. This was brought on at lunch when CJ joined the Glitterati at their table. He sat between Piper and Mandy. So as Joel sat in every class thereafter with his eyes closed and one of his socks draped across his eye lids, and tissue sticking out of each ear, I began to feel guilty. Yes, I was super happy that Joel was distracted by his feelings for Mandy and had forgotten about Frogman. But at what cost? Joel looked and acted weirder than usual and clearly was in pain. He scrunched his eyes and yelped as he climbed up the steps onto our bus. As the school bus swerved, turned, jolted, and bumped along on our route home, Joel held his head as if his brains might explode.

Because of my lingering guilty feelings from the day before, I agreed to join Joel at seven a.m. on Saturday morning in the middle of the woods. Artie came along too. We stood on the banks of my pond. Well, I don't own it and neither do my parents, but I claim it because no one enjoys swimming in its slime more than me. The algae, mud, and dead leaves combine to make the most awesome sludge. It was well worth waking up for in the early fall light. For a moment, I envied Ranger as he ran along the muddy shore with his blue toenails sinking deep into the muck. But then he quickly changed course and sniffed around my shoes.

"Ranger really likes you. I never see him sniffing anyone else the way he sniffs around you. Either that, or you have stinky fish feet." Joel almost smiled at his own joke.

"What are we doing here anyway? I say we go back to my house and eat waffles." Artie yawned so wide I could see his back molars.

"We are looking for clues, evidence. Duh..." Joel snapped back, thrashing dead cattails with a stick.

Artie gave me a look that meant, "What did I do?"

"Ok, where do you want us to start?" I tried to be a helpful friend. Besides I hadn't been out here in weeks. There was no reason to worry he would find anything connecting me to "Frogman."

"You know, footprints or weird pieces of animal remains that he didn't finish eating."

Artie covered his mouth trying not to gag. "It's a little early for half-chewed animals this morning, isn't it?"

"It's not just animal remains we're looking for... you know, scat. Maybe he's shed his skin, so we might find little scraps of that too." Joel was analyzing each and every square inch of mud.

Artie came up beside me. He pushed Ranger away with his foot as if Ranger would eavesdrop and report back to Joel. "Okay, tell me straight up. Are we going to find half-eaten rats, raccoons and the like out here, and have you, you know... gone in the woods? Please tell me no. I am not bagging your poop. In fact, I am not bagging poop period." Artie looked me dead in the eye.

"No, I haven't been out here since Joel made Frogman an internet sensation. I have to take baths in the middle of the night now. Believe me, I would rather swim in that...," I pointed to the middle of the algae covered pond, "then take a bath at home. He's not going to find anything."

Then under my favorite tree where I had spent many happy nights croaking along with a chorus of my webbed toed kin, I saw a dried-out footprint of mine. It wasn't too deep nor was it well-defined, but it was there.   I peered around the tree to see where Joel was and made sure I was out of his eye-line. He made his way around the other side of the pond, so I had but a moment to do what must be done before I was directly across from him. I dug into the dirt with my tip of my shoe marring the top layer of dirt then dragged my heel back across the print. A few more jabs into the dirt with the tip of my shoe and the webbed traces of my nights at the pond were gone. I looked around to be sure there were no other prints when Joel called to me across the pond.

"Find anything? You look like you found something?" Joel stood directly across the pond.

"Uh, no... just poking with my foot to see what was under these dead leaves. Nothing much. Just dirt." Joel stared at me a few more seconds to see what I might do. I quickly looked up into the tree, acting as if there might be a real possibility of a clue hanging off a branch. Joel shook his head at my attempt of scientific study as I sniffed a cluster of Spanish moss that hung low on a twig. He quickly moved on, inspecting the algae and dried leaves that collected at the water's edge.

Frantically, I looked for more of my freaky foot prints around this same tree when the snap of a twig interrupted my search. At first, I thought Ranger had come back to snuffle around my shoes again. But, when I turned around, Ranger was nowhere to be found. In fact, Ranger was trailing behind Joel on the other side of the pond. Another crack of a branch turned my attention deep into the woods. I scanned the trees but there was no one or thing in sight. The sound was loud and close, and there was no way that it was a squirrel or opossum. Whatever caused those branches to break weighed far more than Ranger. He walked across sticks without the slightest snap. No, the only ones who were out here making much noise at all were the three of us.

I squinted and looked between the trees. I gave my best, fake cough, thinking if it was a deer, it would run away. It didn't move. I had the most eerie feeling that I was being watched - that we were being watched and that whatever it was, it was not friendly. It was not pleasant. I had an overwhelming feeling of doom. I had the most horrible thought. What if Joel was right? What if Bigfoot was alive and well roaming our county? What if Bigfoot loved paddling around this pond as much as I did? What if Bigfoot hadn't had breakfast yet and was planning to eat my face with a side of scrambled eggs? I could feel a scream surging inside of me. I reached down, never taking my eyes of the woods and felt around, picking up the heaviest rock within my reach. Standing up, I gripped it, then winding my arm back I threw the rock toward the noise into the trees.

I saw a flash of brown fur. Then I heard screams. Horrible Screams, but they weren't my screams. Did Bigfoot scream like this? I could see branches move and small trees shake. The screaming faded further back into the woods. Artie and Joel came running to my side. Ranger barked and ran back and forth to the tree line, but never ventured forth into the woods to chase "it" down.

"What did you see? What was it?" Artie was pulling on my arm leading me back the way we came. "Let's get out of here."

"Sounds kinda like a wounded coyote." Joel reached out seizing Artie by his coat sleeve preventing him from running. He grabbed my jacket from behind and pulled me back too.

"Before we all freak out, what exactly did you see? Let's all take a walk back to where the initial event occurred." Joel was calm. He pulled out a pad and pencil from his jacket pocket and flipped open his pad. He walked us back to my favorite tree, pushing us forward with the tip of his pencil in our backs. "Is this where you were, about here?" Joel examined the depression in the dirt where I had gouged the dirt with my shoe.

"Yeah, I was around here?" I wasn't too worried. The footprint was long gone.

"What was here? Did you do this?" Joel looked at me as if I had spray-painted Mount Rushmore. It's clear he takes this way too seriously. I need to find him another hobby—and fast.

"I don't know. Nothing was there, just dirt. I guess I was a little bored until I saw something hairy back in those trees." I pointed in the direction of where I saw and heard the terrible "it."

Joel took another look around as if trying to memorize each and every leaf, twig and patch of dirt in its place. "Okay, you two stay here and I'll go in. Just don't touch anything. Got it? Just stand here and wait for me." As he disappeared into the tree line, he admonished us one last time with a loud whisper, "Don't touch a thing!"

It was clear Joel considered this an active crime scene. For all I knew, Joel believed me to be a person of interest. I didn't exactly like the way he'd been looking at me.

"What if he never comes back? How long do we wait?" Artie's hand was twitching and he was looking about the trees like a wild man. "Maybe we should stand back to back in case we're attacked."

Artie had a good point. Though we would most likely not be attacked by Ninjas, how were we to know if Bigfoots were not indeed the Ninjas of the forest? It seemed like a smart idea. Artie and I stood back to back. I listened so hard for Joel's return that I could hear my heart beat in my ears. After what seemed like hours, Joel came crashing through the brush.

"Well, if something was there. It's not there now." Joel brushed off leaves from his jacket. "So what exactly did you see and hear?" Joel returned to his pad and pencil.

I told him the truth, minus my footprint. I told him how I felt like we were being watched, and how it was an overwhelming eerie feeling. It was like a feeling of creepiness mixed with a bit of anger. I asked if Bigfoots were irritable. That's when Artie shot me a look like it was very wrong of me to encourage Joel in this Bigfoot nonsense.

"Well, I guess if we were invading their territory they would not be happy about it. I assume coming between an adult Bigfoot and its young would be quite dangerous. You're sure you saw fur? Actual hair?" Joel was still writing on his notepad.

"Yes, brown fur. Absolutely."

"Not scales, not leathery skin, not froggish looking spots?" Joel inquired again making sure I had not been mistaken.

"No, it was definitely hairy. It had to have been big. It was cracking branches and twigs."

"Did it have large teeth, fangs, or tusks?" Joel was still writing notes.

Now all I could think was, "Do Bigfoots have tusks?" I could have died. I wanted to jump home. Joel didn't appear afraid at all. Instead, he slowly leaned over and patted Ranger on the head.

"Maybe what you saw was a wild hog, a feral pig? How tall was it?" Joel scratched Ranger behind his ear.

"Somewhat tall, not a pig...Let's go home and discuss this over breakfast. I'm getting hungry." I tried to mask my fear with my immediate need of pancakes. I wondered if crickets tasted good with berries and syrup.

"Yeah, let's get some breakfast." Artie said, He was freaked out as well. "There's nothing here except that creepy creature in the woods and it's not Frogman, so I say we go eat. If there were prints we would have found them already." Joel surveyed the pond one last time, put his pad and pencil in his coat pocket and we turned back to go home.

Chapter Eleven

Libby was already on her fourth piece of gum when we sat down for breakfast. Mom was quick to set out orange juice and milk. Soon we were all enjoying her buckwheat pancakes. Her secret ingredients are vanilla and cinnamon. One day I am going to add my secret ingredient of mealworms. Sam came to the table and chowed down with us. He, however, was talking with his mouth open. Artie, Joel and I cringed watching Sam devour his breakfast. For a second, I wished we were back in the woods.

Dad read the paper and sipped his coffee quietly. Mom brought a platter stacked with pancakes to the table and sat down to join us. That's when any thought of a crazed, tusked, hairy beast in the woods vanished like the last bits of breakfast on Artie's plate. We were all going back for seconds when someone rang the doorbell. It was 8:30 in the morning, a little too early for visitors.

Libby looked at the door and then back at me, "Well…. aren't you going to get it?"

"You can answer the door as easily as I can." I stuffed another piece of pancake into my mouth.

The doorbell rang again.

"Ummmm, it's your turn to get IT…" Libby scowled, unwrapping another piece of gum. Of course, she was talking to me, but Artie jumped up and ran to the door.

In seconds, a flailing, screeching, delirious lunatic was raving on the front door step. Artie stepped back from the torrent of hysterical cries and revealed our early morning visitor. Katie. She held her upper left arm while she shrieked threats at me. "I'm calling the police and you're going to jail. Then I'm going to sue you and then my big brother is going to beat you up for what you did!"

My mom was at the door when Katie broke down into more howls. Within two more seconds, I was a goner.

"Alex! You threw at rock at Katie? Go to your room!"

"I didn't throw a rock at Katie!"

Dad glowered at me, stood from his chair, and escorted me to the front door. Katie wore a beige jacket with brown faux fur that trimmed her hoodie. She still held her arm. But behind her was the more shocking revelation; CJ Dillon, and he looked as angry as a pranked grizzly bear who woke up wearing eye shadow and lipstick. From behind me I could hear Joel choking on his orange juice.

"What's this all about?" Dad brought Katie and CJ inside our home. We were being invaded.

"He threw a huge rock at me, on purpose! It hurts!" Katie broke out into sobs again. CJ stood by popping his knuckles.

"I don't know what she's talking about. I didn't hurt her. I didn't throw a rock..." my mind instantly flashed to our morning in the woods.

"Liar. You're a big, fat liar!" Katie hissed in between sobs.

"Did you follow us into the woods this morning?" I asked as kindly as I could so that I wouldn't provoke the bear standing behind her.

She wouldn't answer us at first. She kept crying as Mom urged her to take off her jacket so she could see the wound.

"Dad, it's not what you're thinking. Artie, Joel and I went down to the pond this morning to take a look around. I heard some rustling in the woods. I saw some fur and thought it was a large, you know…"

CJ broke out laughing. He was whooping and snorting hysterically and pointing at Katie. He could barely speak, but finally managed, "You thought Katie was some kind of rabid raccoon that was going to gnaw your face. That's so funny. You're afraid of a third grader! You're more pathetic than I thought!"

Mom and Dad gave a very disappointed look at CJ. They don't condone name calling or negative commentary.

"That's not what happened." I tried to defend myself.

"They were looking for that stupid Frogman." Katie sneered. She was no longer crying now that my mom was bandaging her arm.

"You were following us." I really needed to put some of the blame squarely on Katie. If she hadn't been following us, then I wouldn't have winged a rock at her. At the same time, I was also glad to know that Bigfoot was not hanging around my subdivision. For all I know Bigfoot eats frogs.

"Was not." Katie stuck out her tongue at me as soon as my mom turned around.

"Alex, please apologize to Katie." Mom put a second band aid on Katie's arm.

"What? Me. Apologize?"

"Yes, and now." Mom gave me that look that meant, "Do what I am asking you or I will send you off to a cauliflower farm in Siberia without the internet, or video games."

I did what I had to do. I caved. Besides my dad was standing beside me staring me down with steely eyeballs over his reading glasses. I apologized for throwing a rock into the tree line. I didn't mean to hit her.

Katie seemed to accept my apology. It was hard to tell. She nodded at me and sniffled, but there was still a look of mistrust in her eyes. CJ on the other hand stifled a laugh. Then my mom did the unthinkable. She invited them to breakfast.

Joel dropped his fork on his plate with a metallic crash. Artie gaped with half-chewed pancake hanging out of his mouth. Sam looked like someone had eaten the very last piece of bacon on the planet. CJ and Katie, surprisingly, accepted my mom's offer of breakfast.

CJ and Katie sat next to Libby who was chewing her fifth piece of gum of the morning. Katie gave Libby a sorrowful look, eyeing her pack of gum next to her glass of orange juice. Libby rolled her eyes in the most dramatic fashion possible and relented. Katie, pleased with herself, folded the piece of gum into her mouth and began chewing triumphantly.

Mom returned to the kitchen to pour more pancake batter on the griddle. Dad left the table with his paper. The seven of us sat around the kitchen table in silence. Joel wriggled in his chair and gripped his fork. I worried that Joel might challenge CJ to a duel; a duel of forks and slabs of butter. Either way, it would not be pretty. It was Sam, though, who took matters into his own hands. He blew a raspberry at Katie. In reply, Katie spit out her piece of gum into her hand and plopped it onto what was left of Sam's breakfast.

"Frogman is so stupid! There is no Frogman!" Katie yelped. "Everyone knows Frogmen don't exist. I bet you believe in..."

"Here we are, more pancakes..." Mom was using her sing-song voice to calm things down. "Who needs more juice?"

Sam and Katie both held up their glasses and Mom quickly poured orange juice until their glasses were full.

Mom must have sensed how tense we all were at the table because she began to ask Katie and CJ the usual questions any adult asks a kid. "How is school? How do you like your teachers? Are you settling into your new home alright? Wow. Thursday night's game was really terrific. How do you feel about the game, CJ?"

Good manners dictated that I should remain at the table until CJ and Katie had finished eating. All I wanted was to be anywhere but here, having breakfast with THEM. Joel still had a firm grip on his fork and Artie's eyelids took turns twitching. I imagined that, for Joel, sharing breakfast with CJ was a worse nightmare than to find out Bigfoots were really overgrown bunnies.

In between bites of pancake, CJ went on and on about how he did this and that to win the game. He hoped Coach Finley learned that he should start each game as quarterback. Joel clamped down on his spoon with his free hand and still held the fork in the other.

"Hey, maybe you kids could go play basketball while I make some oatmeal cookies. You can stay as long as you like. I know your mom is at work this morning...Lots going on and all." Mom was trying so hard for us all to be friends.

"Thank you, Mrs. Addison, but we really should be going. I need to rest my arm anyway. Thank you for breakfast." CJ looked at Katie and cocked his head towards the front door. We collectively breathed a sigh of relief. They were two steps from the front door when Mom did the unthinkable.

"Tell your mom 'hello' for me. Hey, if your family is staying in town this Thanksgiving, you are welcome to spend it with us. Have your mom give me a call. Bye."

Chapter Twelve

Joel immediately gagged as if he was overcome by an infestation of stinkbugs. Artie remained calm. I think I forgot to breathe. Then my thoughts zoomed as to what could come next. Would Mom not rest until we were committed to a gift exchange with CJ's family this Christmas? I could see it now, all of us opening gifts together on Christmas morning. I would be CJ's Secret Santa. This is horrrrrrrible!

Mom walked back into the kitchen to clean up, humming through her ginormous smile. I finally gasped for air. I couldn't understand why she felt this was the best idea ever, when it was really the worst.

"Mom, what did you just do? Why would you invite THEM for Christmas???!!!!???" I demanded, pointing my fork in her direction.

"Come on. That's quite enough!" She snapped back at me. "They are new to this community. They don't know anyone else. Be NICE!"

There was no arguing with her. She clearly has forgotten the dreaded experience of middle school and bullies.

Artie snapped his fingers in front of my eyes until I focused solely on him.

"Hey, this isn't the end of the world. You'll be fine and the world will be safe once again, just as soon as Katie and CJ realize that your mom cooks a tofurkey instead of a real turkey. There's no chance that CJ is going to eat tofu, ever. He may eat your soul, but never tofu. Got it? You're good."

This is why Artie is my best friend. He is always quick to point out the obvious, like my Mom's avoidance of cooking real food that's actually meat. She thinks it's best to eat a diet of vegetables and plants, even on holidays that were created for eating meat and gravy.

We cleared the kitchen table as fast as we could and ran to my room. Joel grabbed one of my pillows off my bed and bit down on it. He tried to control an undeniable urge to scream and yell. I knew how he felt. To have CJ invade our school was one thing, but now he had breached the walls of my fortress - the

Addison household. Our very freedom and security was now in question. Clearly, we were under attack.

Joel finally unhinged his teeth from my pillow and began to speak. He tried his hardest to remain calm. "I think we should let your mom know that it would be best to throw away the dishes CJ used. I don't think any amount of hot water and detergent will rid her plate and flatware of his awful genetic code. I mean, how can we positively know if his condition is contagious or not? Who, here, wants to be a flimflammer, pretender, and fraud?"

Joel got more dramatic by the second. Even though I wasn't exactly sure what a flimflammer was, I could bet it wasn't good. I could also bet that throwing away my mom's dishes would earn me twenty-seven years of washing her new dishes, every day until my fingers shriveled off my hands.

"We're not throwing away my mom's dishes. Like Artie pointed out, all we have to do is let CJ know how much my mom loves to cook up tasteless food and he'll never bother us again. I say we just try to stay as far away from him as we can."

"He may not come for Thanksgiving, but he knows where you live. He could come over every day, just to hang out. You don't know what he's capable of." Joel shivered and bit down on my pillow again.

That afternoon was our basketball team's first practice. Artie and I rode with his dad, Mr. Brandt, to our school's gym at 2:30. He and Coach Swanson lined us up and then asked us to take a seat on the gym floor. Mr. Brandt went down the line introducing himself and meeting each player. He then went into a 5 minute speech about one of the most important aspects of the game. "Games are won because of a little known secret and yet it is often taken for granted.

Divisions, Conferences, and National Championships are won because of this one "thing." Mr. Brandt was really throwing around air-quotes, but we didn't care. We were riveted to the gym floor, each of us wanting to desperately know this secret. "This 'thing' will become second nature. It will change your life," he continued on. "It's so important, and some of you have been doing it wrong for years." We all gulped. We had no idea what he was talking about. "I do not want us losing a game because you did not listen. I do not want us losing a game because you did not make the changes necessary to win! Are you with me?" He pounded his fist into his palm. We all hooted and clapped our hands. It was so exciting. Mr. Brandt was going to lead us into a new life as victors, as basketball prodigies. "Who wants to know what my secret to winning is? Who wants to know? Raise your hand if you want to be a winner!" We all shot our hands high into the air.

"Good, I'm glad to see it. Everyone come in close," he motioned for us to sit in a semi-circle at his feet. We settled down around him, leaning in to hear words that were going to change our life forever.

"It's your shoelaces. Every one of you needs to know how to properly tie your shoes. It makes all the difference in the world."

Wait? What? Did I hear him correctly?

"Artie, come here and demonstrate for us." Mr. Brandt clapped his hands together once again.

To say that the team felt a little deflated to hear that the secret to winning was shoelaces would be an understatement. The only thing I could think was maybe the NBA sold magical shoelaces that were handmade by Michael Jordan. Artie, for his part, stood in front of the team next to his dad. He was red in the face, as his dad leaned over and pulled on his laces and the tongue of his shoe. "See here guys, this is all wrong, tongue needs to be pulled up all the way and the laces need to be tight." Mr. Brandt pulled on Artie's other shoelaces as Artie was now turning white. I heard snickering as I watched Artie's left eyelid twitch violently. We spent the next ten minutes re-learning how to tie our shoes properly to avoid blisters, because as Mr. Brandt told us, it's hard to win when our feet hurt with ugly, bubbly blisters. Unfortunately, Artie did not appreciate his father's secret to winning. Nor did he appreciate that his dad kept using him as an example of "what not to do."

After practice, Mr. Brandt dropped us off at my house. When his father drove away, Artie collapsed on the lawn. He felt worse than ever before. "I can't believe this, not only can I not shoot, do lay-ups, and free-throws, I find out in front of the whole team that I never learned to tie my shoes properly. You would have thought that my father would have taught me that "secret" when I was in kindergarten. My life is so over. I can't do anything right and now my dad is just going to point it out three times a week in front of an audience."

"I really think he's trying to help you and the rest of us. He probably thought you wouldn't mind being his volunteer."

"Well, maybe I'm such an embarrassment that he won't call on me anymore. There's no way I'm the son he wanted. I bet he'd rather have CJ for a son. Ugh...You're so lucky, Alex." Artie pulled up handfuls of brown grass and threw it into the wind. "You have a regular dad who isn't famous. He's just normal, average, mediocre, and balding."

Hey, I know my dad works hard at the university teaching computer science but now wasn't the time to point out his receding hairline. We went inside and after I ate a handful of bugs, Artie thought maybe his life wasn't so bad after all. At least he doesn't have a taste for insects. I laid in bed that night and talked to God again after everyone had fallen asleep. While Artie had a horrible day at basketball practice, I had come to my own realization about basketball. I told God how I was thankful for the abilities he gave me, but I was also kind of sad that I would never be able to play a real game of basketball; a real game where I could jump and dunk with my new skills. Just like in football, where I couldn't show off how far I could really kick a ball, in basketball there would be no sensational dunks made from across the court. I would always have to play like the 'ME' before I became Frogman. Then as I was about to finish my prayer with a silent "amen," God reminded me, Frogman or not, I still had work to do on my three pointers. I fell asleep looking forward to our next practice.

Sunday morning we were all at church raiding the table full of donuts. By all, I mean me, Sam, Libby, Joel and Artie. Joel had insisted on spending the night to provide round the clock security in case CJ tried to come over to my house again. Artie spent the night to make sure Joel didn't go spider monkey on CJ in case he did decide to return. It would probably take the two of us to keep Joel from inciting CJ into a duel of fists. Joel is scrappy but CJ has all the advantages.

The donut table at my church is a heavenly sight. Mrs. Wilkins, God bless her for her doughnut shop, covers this popular table with trays of sprinkled and glazed doughnuts. You have to come early or you are left with the sad residue that has dripped and dribbled across the surface of the trays. At this point, you have one option; to scrap your finger across the platter for any slight bit of gooey goodness that might be left.

That's a real bummer.

We had come to church early, so it was our good fortune to have first pick of Mrs. Wilkins sugary pastries. It was a flurry of hands and fingers as we reached in to grab our favorite doughnut when Mom pulled me back from the table. I barely held onto my chocolate doughnut when Mom whispered into my ear, "Hey honey, let our guests go first." I looked at my mom in confusion. Artie's family attend our church. Joel has been here so many times that he's actually on our class roster. Mom, ever so subtly, nodded her head to the right. Over her shoulder stood CJ and his family.

I dropped my doughnut but I didn't care, I had to get Joel away from the table without him noticing CJ. I grabbed Joel by the arm and led him down the hall toward our classroom. I could see that Artie was already aware of the situation. He was pale white as he walked behind Joel to block his view in case he turned around for any reason.

Once our Sunday school class started, Nate was all too happy to meet CJ and introduce him to the rest of the class. Nate loves visitors but he was already familiar with CJ. He had been at the game Thursday night. Nate couldn't stop grinning as he talked with CJ about his remarkable debut. Joel nearly threw up his sprinkles. Things didn't get much better after that, especially when my mom insisted that CJ's family sit with us during the sermon. Artie immediately plopped down next to Libby, Joel squeezed in on the other side between Artie and Sam, which left me on the end—next to CJ. I don't think CJ goes to church much. He spent a lot of time cracking his knuckles, smacking his gum and looking at his shoes. I don't think there is anything interesting about brown laces.

Driving home, Dad asked what we had learned at church and Joel muttered that our sanctum sanctorum had been invaded.

"Oh, so you were studying the Roman empire?" My dad was really interested.

"Nope," Joel grumbled.

"Huh?" Dad and Mom both glanced back at Joel but he smiled as pleasantly as he could for both of them. After Dad and Mom's attention were back on the road, Joel whispered to Artie and me, "This is not a drill. I repeat, not a drill. It's GO time."

Yes, it was a bit uncomfortable to sit with CJ in church when I know perfectly well that he can't stand me or my friends. However, uncomfortable, I can live with. It's what happened the following Tuesday afternoon that I can live without.

Chapter Thirteen

Tuesday was Veteran's Day and Mom took us to watch our community's parade down Main street. This is a big day for Mom since the Historical Society has its own float. Even if she had two broken legs, and only one thumb, nothing would stop her from driving that float. Libby, Sam and I are always happy to help in any way we can because, as Mom has not figured out yet, this is the best day of the year for candy, after Halloween, of course. Every year we stand near the front of the crowd to collect as much chocolate as we can while it is flung from costumed people and soldiers in the parade. The trick is to eat it all before Mom comes back around to take us home.

That afternoon, after the parade had ended, and I was on a sugar high, Artie and Joel came over to shoot hoops. In the driveway, Joel jumped up and down—tripping over his words. He was still so excited about his upcoming interview for "Beast T.V." I hadn't seen him this excited in a long time, not since he first watched "The Legend of Boggy Creek." Of course, after he watched this classic movie about a Bigfoot attack in Arkansas, he had nightmares for weeks. Still, he was hooked, and this movie only served as more confirmation that he was hot on the trail of this legendary beast.

Suddenly, my guts began to knot and I had a horrid feeling. What if Joel had two reasons to be excited? What if Joel had worked all night long on a plan to bring CJ down? What if he wanted me to be a part of it? What if Joel thought he could trap CJ the way he is trying to capture Bigfoot – with a jar of peanut butter and a chocolate candy bar? We'll be laughed out of sixth grade.

"You're not going to believe what happened yesterday..." Joel was still hopping from one foot to another.

Artie leaned in to hear. I took a step back. I was sure that Joel was going to lay out his master plan to annoy CJ with an exploding peanut butter filled football.

"My very favorite wildlife geneticist from Washington State University messaged me late last night. He has been following the "Frogman" story. He is now going to be a part of the same episode as me! AND, he wants me to come and speak at their regional conference in the Spring! Apparently two of my other favorite wildlife biologists spoke with him about inviting me. Isn't this just the best news ever?!? You know, I could bring my new evidence to the conference. I've got so much to do to prepare for it. The month of May will be here before you know it!" In his excitement, Joel threw the ball up at the hoop and it went flying into the neighbor's yard. He went bounding across the lawn to retrieve the ball and was quickly out of earshot.

"I think we need to find out what this new piece of evidence is that Joel is going to expose to the world. We don't have much time," Artie's eye twitched.

"Yeah, it must be good or that "Beast T.V." guy wouldn't be coming here. I have to convince Joel to spill his secret before tomorrow."

Later that night as I was perusing Joel's Facelook page looking for any clue to this new evidence he held, I consoled myself with the fact that even with this other piece of evidence, he still didn't know of my involvement. Artie and I had tried everything to get Joel to give me a clue as to what he had on "Frogman." I even offered to invite Mandy to sit with us at lunch. Joel wouldn't budge. He kept telling me and Artie that we would have to wait just like the rest of the world.

So, there I was scanning his posts looking for any trace of myself within his updates when I heard my mom yelping from the living room. I jumped up and ran to the living room thinking that my mom was being attacked by a badger. But it was just the television. In fact, it was CJ's mom, Jackie Dillon on the ten o'clock news. She stood at a podium and the subtitles below her image read, "Cedarville Press Conference, Jackie Dillion, Public Information Officer, Cedarville Police, Investigation continues on mysterious creature at Marshall House Fire." CJ's mom finished up and took questions from reporters. Light bulbs flashed. Police Chief Bob Carlton stepped up to the podium to update the press on the investigation.

"I would like to first thank my officers and the Texas Rangers in their support and efforts in this on-going investigation. After many hours of investigation, I have come to the conclusion that Cedarville has an unidentified creature roaming its hillsides. I am asking the public to take extreme caution. Please be aware of your surroundings at all times. Keep children near you. Children should be indoors by nightfall. If you have seen what appears to be some sort of strange, scary being or animal, or have any information concerning this situation, please call our new toll-free hotline, 1-800-555-3764. Please, do not approach it. It is believed to be dangerous. The safety of this community is our number one priority. Thank you."

The camera cut to our local news reporter, Kelly Meadows, who then summed up the Police Press Conference, but added her own flair by ending the segment with, "Please use caution when outdoors, going to school, work, and home. And if you have any information regarding Cedarville's monster, please call

1-800-555-3764. Again, we have been advised to not approach this monster as it may be quite dangerous." I was shocked. How could they think that about me?

Mom and Dad sat looking at the television, stunned into silence. I stood behind them, looking at my hands, my arms, and then reached up and felt my face. Just because I really like eating insects does not mean I am a monster. Dad turned off the television with the remote but it was my mom who was first to speak.

"Are all the doors locked, the windows, and the garage door? Everything?" Mom stood up and checked the windows in the living room. I numbly got up, dazed as I walked back to my room. I went to bed as Mom and Dad checked every window and door. Then my mom went through the house one more time and rechecked everything again. Everyone was soon asleep, but me. I couldn't stop thinking how I was now under investigation. Everyone is to be cautious around me. I would never hurt anyone. All I did was save Piper and Dirk from that fire on Halloween night.

Wednesday morning, by my locker, Joel walked up dragging his backpack behind him. He looked like he hadn't slept a wink all night either.

"Joel, are you all right? Today's your big day and you look like..." I was cut off by Artie.

"Like a zombie! What's wrong with you? Why are you wearing a shirt with cornflakes stuck to it for your interview?" Artie pointed out a clump of cereal that was resting in one of his shirt's wrinkles. And sweatpants too? Do you really want to be filmed like this?

"It doesn't matter. They called last night and have postponed the interview...indefinitely."

"What does that mean?" I really wanted to know. Were my worries now over?

"It means that something is going on and I have no idea. It can't be good, that I'm sure of. The producers were all set to come and interview me and premiere my new evidence. They went back and forth, texting my parents and then 12 hours ago, it all just stopped. Something is definitely wrong. My parents made me come to school and all I want to do is contact Soren Bergman and find out what's going on. It's so unfair being a kid!" Joel stormed off to class with breakfast still stuck to his shirt.

"At least your identity hasn't been blown," Artie grinned.

"Oh, well they may not know it's me, but on the news last night, CJ's mom and the Police Chief issued warnings about me and called me a monster," I said with a half-hearted laugh. "I mean, c'mon, it's me. I'm not a monster."

108

"CJ's mom was on television? Why?" Artie asked.

"That's all that you heard me say, really? She works for the police department. She was part of the press conference and they called me a monster." I was becoming annoyed.

"So… you mean, with CJ's mom working with the police, CJ could really be an undercover agent or he's really not a sixth grader like Joel thinks. Interesting…"

"For real, that's what you're focusing on? They said that I was dangerous and a MONSTER," I whispered as loudly as I could so that Artie could hear my frustration but no one else would.

"That's just nuts. They have no idea, what you are. I will admit that it's super gross that you eat bugs, but you're not a zombie. Just don't do anything for a while and this will all go away. It's like the press with my father. He quit playing basketball and eventually the media attention stopped. It's easy. Don't do anything."

And he was right. To not do anything would be easy. I just have to not do anything. My day was looking up and incredibly so was Joel's.

During P.E. was when Joel's wish for CJ's downfall came true, or at least that's when Joel heard the good news. In the locker room after the game last Thursday night, CJ made himself obnoxiously annoying to Coach Finley and the rest of the coaching staff and team. He repeatedly congratulated himself out-loud on winning the game for everyone. He chest-bumped Todd Highfield and then stood on a bench and howled.

Coach Finley must not be a fan of howling, self-congratulatory speeches, and reckless towel-snapping. To everyone's surprise, including Todd and CJ, Coach Finley announced that Dirk the Jerk would be running the first team offense this Thursday night. Artie was a bit confused since he knew more about basketball, so I whispered to him while we were doing push-ups, "Dirk the Jerk is going to be the starting quarterback." Artie's elbows folded and he collapsed onto the floor.

"What?"

"It's true. Take a look at Dirk." I whispered back.

Artie and I looked over at Dirk. Despite the sweat on his brow, he was smiling. Dirk looked over at CJ, smirked, and then kept right on doing his push-ups. Within seconds every guy had stopped exercising as we watched Dirk the Jerk and CJ battle it out for the most push–ups in class. Dirk kept pace with CJ. Smiling like he was doing nothing more than eating a cookie, CJ watched Dirk for any signs of fatigue. When Dirk began to slow ever so slightly, CJ snorted a laugh. Dirk fell further behind and with two more push-ups, it was over. CJ had beaten Dirk. CJ jumped to his feet and went over to Dirk, extending his hand out to him. Dirk, like the rest of us, figured he offered a gesture of good will by helping him up. Just when Dirk reached back, CJ laughed, turned away and walked back to the locker room. I looked around the gym. Coach McGrath was nowhere to be seen and no other adult was within sight. CJ was clearly messing with Dirk. Kevin and Randy dashed to Dirk's side. Kevin reached out his hand to help pull Dirk up but Dirk got to his feet on his own.

"I don't know who to root for?" Artie said shaking his head.

"This is unexpected." Joel muttered as he joined us from two rows over.

"Who knew I would ever take Dirk's side? It seemed impossible, but could CJ be a bigger jerk than Dirk? After all these years, I was now rooting for Dirk— hoping he would have a better game than CJ."

Later that day near the end of school, Principal Evans made an announcement over the loud speaker. "Excuse me for this interruption but we have a lost piece of gym equipment. If anyone has seen a whistle on a blue cord, please bring it to the office. I repeat, we have a lost silver whistle on a blue cord..." At this point we could hear muffled talking in the background. Principal Evans must have put his hand over the microphone. After a few protestations with a loud, raised voice and several coughs, Principal Evans spoke over the intercom system once again. "I have been informed that there will be a reward. If you find it, please return it to the school office. Thank you."

Chapter Fourteen

After school as I waited for my bus to arrive, I noticed Coach McGrath standing by the outside doors. He smiled at each student as they passed through the doors and waved goodbye.

"That's so weird. I wonder if he hit his head and is suffering a concussion." Joel looked at Coach McGrath as if he was scientifically studying him.

"Yeah, he never cares if we make our buses or not at the end of the day. Besides, he should be at the field getting ready for seventh and eighth grade football practice." Artie said as he stepped onto our bus.

I took my seat by the window and as the bus rolled away, I could swear that Coach McGrath was clinching his teeth behind his smile.

Once I was home, I ran to my bedroom and grabbed my hidden box of dead bugs from out of my closet. There was only one left. I popped it into my mouth, savoring this last treat, and changed into sweats for basketball practice. I really needed to go by the pet store for more crickets in the next few days, because I had absolutely cleaned my house of dead flies and spiders. As I waited in the living room for Mom to drive me to practice, I was annoyed to see that shesawqqqqq was cleaning off the dining table and setting out coffee cups.

"Mom, what are you doing? I'm going to be late."

"Oh, your dad is coming home any minute to take you to practice."

I was surprised to see Dad home so early on a Wednesday afternoon. He took me to basketball practice and like everyone else, got to witness Artie tie his shoes properly, miss free throws, trip and fall over his feet as we dribbled up and down the court, and get humiliated by CJ. It was crushing for Artie. CJ came in off the football field to use the bathroom when he saw Artie's dad coaching our team. We were practicing free throws when Artie's ball ricocheted off the backboard and rolled to where CJ was standing at half-court. Looking at the ball and then at Artie, he smiled and sent the ball swooshing through the net. Artie's dad ran over with a huge grin on his face and high-fived CJ. Artie's dad completely ignored the rest of us while he and CJ took turns shooting baskets at the other end of the court. Artie's dad praised CJ right and left. With each compliment for CJ's basketball skills, Artie shrunk one incher lower. With hunching shoulders, Artie finally walked off the court and waited outside.

It was bad. What made it worse was how Mr. Brandt didn't even notice that Artie had left. Most of the time, Artie likes to be invisible, but not like this, and not when your own dad doesn't see you too.

My dad drove Artie and me home. It was a long ride. No one spoke. Even my father knew not to try to break the silence with upbeat silliness, and advice. As Artie exited the car, my dad said, "It won't always be like this. It gets better, I promise. Come over some time and I will tell you about a kid who had such a horrible speech impediment that he couldn't say his own name correctly until the third grade, and now he talks for a living. I've got loads of stories!"

"Thank you, Mr. Addison." Artie started to shut the door.

"Trust me," my dad smiled. Artie nodded, shut the door and trudged across his lawn and into his house.

I felt bad for Artie, but once I was home, I would have switched places with him in an instant. I walked through the front door and immediately was overwhelmed by the commotion of 40 women and seven men talking all at once. They were crammed into our living room. It was standing room only. Even Artie's mom was here. My mom stood on our hearth and banged a wooden spoon against a cheese grater. She really needed something bigger, like the Liberty Bell. She waved her arms around as if she were trying to fly away, then the adults quieted down. Dad whispered to stay out of the living room and to keep Sam out of the way too. I walked through the crowd and found Sam. I told him that if he was good, I would let him finish off the carob chip ice cream as long as he let me listen in on this impromptu meeting.

Sam sat on the kitchen counter, ice cream dribbling down his chin and fingers. He was a mess, but a quiet mess as he silently ate his way to the bottom of the ice cream container. I sneaked my way to the back of the meeting, keeping one eye on Sam. Mom talked about being united, diligent, aware, and proactive. Everyone clapped in agreement. Then she introduced someone from our community who was there to help; someone who would lead the way. Someone who had an inside scoop into this terrible situation we all faced. It was CJ's mom, Jackie Dillon.

Everyone hushed as she stepped onto the hearth. She began to tell everyone not to over-react, then proceeded to tell everyone that what our community faced was no doubt one of the most alarming situations to ever hit any community since recorded history. What we faced was unknown, dangerous, probably lethal, and it was imperative that

116

a neighborhood watch be formed. If we didn't work together, someone could get seriously hurt or die. Ellen, my mom, would lead the neighborhood watch and all meetings would now take place at our home, now known as Command Central.

According to CJ's mom: there were 5 things our community was up against:

1. There was an unknown and undocumented animal/monster that is most likely hostile, dangerous, and hungry. We don't even know what this thing eats yet. It appears it might not have been saving the children. It might have been looking for an easy meal.

2. We must keep children and pets indoors. Only allow children and pets outdoors when necessary. Parents will take turns standing guard at all bus stops in the morning and afternoon.

3. A curfew for children will be in place at sunset. No children are allowed outside after dark unless escorted by a parent or guardian.

4. We must put up flyers around town with the new monster hotline telephone number and a picture of the monster.

5. Again, we must remember this is an undocumented species. We don't know where it lives and what it eats... Do not try to approach it. Call 911

or the hotline. Don't risk being a hero. We have it on good authority that it is very dangerous.

The meeting dispersed, but my heart sank. All I could think was, "who has it on good authority that I am dangerous? Does someone know something about me that I don't know? Why do they keep referring to me as a monster?"

Thursday morning Artie reminded me to lay low until everything blows over. "Remember, just do nothing. It's easy. Nothing." But not taking action still didn't ease my mind.

"I can't believe everyone, including my parents, thinks that I am a monster?" I rolled my eyes.

"Yeah, I have to say that my mom and dad are now seriously concerned. My mom even checked the closets and under the beds last night before any of us went to sleep. Don't worry everyone will get over this soon." Artie put his hand on my shoulder reassuringly.

"I don't think you would have eaten Dirk. That's just way too gross!"

"Think? Think...? You could have said, 'I know you wouldn't have eaten Dirk.' Are you doubting me?"

"No, no, not at all. Hey I didn't mean it like that. It's going to work out."

Joel showed up to class looking like a cast member from a horror film that was about the living dead. He was wearing the same clothes he wore yesterday and by all appearances he slept in them too. His hair looked like it had been styled by an angry gorilla. There were traces of strawberry danish on his shirt. The smeared strawberry gave the added effect that he had fought off the living dead but had barely won. Sometime in the last two days, he must have misplaced his deodorant too. He stank.

"Are you all right. What happened?" I was genuinely concerned.

Joel put fresh water in Fluffy's aquarium. He looked like he was barely awake. His eyes fluttered. I think the bright lights of the classroom hurt his eyes. "Uhmm, I'm good, I think."

"You don't look good and you don't smell good." I was doing my best to look away from Fluffy. I really didn't want to be anywhere near her, like ever. Luckily, Joel's stench masked her snakey bacony smell.

Joel sniffed his underarms and his eyes popped wiped open. "I wondered where that smell was coming from. I thought the janitor was burning trash in the school somewhere." Joel picked up fluffy and tried to take her back to his seat.

"Yeah, you can't do that," I said trying not to freak. "You have to keep her in her aquarium."

A couple of students howled, "Put her back! What are you doing? Put her back!" The girls were moving towards the door. Lance had one foot in the hallway.

"Oh, right, I forgot where I was," Joel sleepily shrugged, turned around and put her back in her glass cage.

All I could get out of Joel was that he had called and left messages for Soren Bergman but Soren was not returning calls. The producers of Beast T.V. were not returning his calls either. He did mention that he had stayed up all night monitoring some websites and chatting with his pen pal online. I didn't even know he had one. He didn't want to talk about it, except that he thought calling the 'Frogman' a 'monster' this early in the stage of the investigation was absolutely irresponsible. "We don't know what it is. That's why we need biologists and zoologists investigating this, and not just the Texas Rangers." He had heard back from them, and unfortunately they could not get enough detail from his pictures. All they could say about it was that it looked to be covered in some kind of substance, possibly mud. With that, Joel sighed, "I don't know why this is confusing for them or unexpected. I have said all along it's amphibian. Amphibians like water and mud."

Joel continued to sleep through most of the day, even when Dirk lost two of his homework assignments, including a report on World War 1. It represented 10%

of our grade. You might be wondering why I care? It's because I overheard Dirk say that he had to keep his grades up or his parents won't let him play football, no matter what, even if it was the play-offs. I want Dirk to quarterback tonight. He was down two assignments and was searching his backpack and locker. He never found them.

Coach McGrath hadn't found his whistle either. He went all over school looking behind trash bins and under tables. He scoured the gym with two other coaches. Though he was wearing a new shiny, silver whistle with a blue cord, he looked miserable. By the end of the day, he had a bandage around his left thumb. He had accidently stapled it in his office, while putting together a copy of that night's play list for the seventh-grade football team.

During Dirk's last two classes, he sat in the library rewriting his two homework assignments. If he didn't finish—he couldn't play. Randy and Kevin sat with him with open books, helping him finish his work. Fortunately, he remembered most of what he had already written. With twenty minutes to spare, he turned in his homework before school let out for the day. I could tell he was angry. He kept his head down. His hands were fisted as he walked out front to catch the bus. Kevin and Randy flanked him on each side as if trying to protect him and keep him calm. At least he would be quarterbacking the game that night.

Things got weirder at school and at home. The school went on high alert. Five more teachers were outside watching students get on the bus. Actually, they weren't really watching students. The teachers had their own mission. They nervously scanned the tree-line across the street, the fields to the sides of the school building, and up and down the road that runs directly in front of our school. These teachers clutched two-way radios in their hands. Principal Evans, with his walkie-talkie, patrolled the halls of the school at the end of the day, checked in with staff and got feedback on their positions. It was like being in some kind of war movie. Unfortunately, Joel hadn't noticed the military posture of the teachers out front. If he wasn't so sleepy, I think he would have joined them.

A new and strange pattern formed as the bus made its way through my neighborhood. At each and every bus stop, a parent waited to help escort children home. When it was my turn to get off the bus, there was my mom, cellphone in one hand and bear spray in the other. Sam held a flashlight and a toy hammer.

"Everything okay? Everything good at school, and on the bus?" Mom surveyed trees, bushes, and mailboxes.

"Yes, everything went well today, except Joel lost a finger in science class so we dissected it. Other than that, everything was great."

"Wonderful. I'm glad you had a good day. Homework?" Mom approached parked cars as if she were on a SWAT team about to take down a bank robber. She wasn't listening to a word I was saying.

"Nah...I just need to use your credit card to buy a hot air balloon to test wind currents over Slovakia."

"Sounds good. Listen once we get inside, you guys are in for the night. Got it? That's the way it has to be until the police figure this 'thing' out. Okay?" Mom was so intense, I knew there was no way she was going to let me shoot baskets in the driveway. So, I just nodded while Sam stuck his flashlight in his mouth and turned it on.

Once inside, it was apparent how my mom spent her day. A map of our community was spread across our kitchen table and divided into sections with a red pen. Three women pointed at different areas on the map while Jackie moved little flags back and forth across our neighborhood. There were stacks of bright yellow paper at one end of the table and rolls of duct tape crowded the other. The paper stacks were flyers with my picture from the night I rescued Dirk and Piper, plus the new monster hotline number. There was no way anyone would ever guess this photograph was me. It was dark, and mostly out of focus. I could not have been happier.

"Uh, what is this supposed to be? It looks like a big, black, blurry blob." I tried to act concerned.

"Yes, I know, but we have to show people what to look for. It was taken by one of the firemen who was gracious enough to let us use it for free." Mom sighed, as she took a crayon away from Sam who had added a smiley face to several blobs. "We would have liked to have used Joel's pictures, but he has copyright on them," Mom rolled her eyes. "So, we can't use them without his permission."

"The agency he signed with is not cooperative. They want a thousand dollars to use one picture for our flyers. And another thing, his agent sounds just like his older brother," one of the other mom's chimed in.

"Well it's good to see that our young people understand what free enterprise is," said another mom.

Cars pulled in and out of our driveway until ten o'clock that night. It reminded me of planes taking off and landing at an airport. It was constant commotion as the doorbell rang all night. Mom or Dad would answer the door and give a concerned citizen a stack of flyers and a roll of duct tape. By eleven o'clock that night street signs, telephone poles, and chain link fencing had been defaced with a very ambiguous picture of me.

Chapter Fifteen

By Friday, school was a military zone. During second period, the school alarm system went off. This was not a fire or a tornado drill. Nope, this was a new drill, specifically for "monster" invasions. The intercom system turned on with an ear-piercing squeal, then Principal Evans coughed, clearing his throat. "Students in five minutes we will be conducting a new safety drill. Please follow instructions given by your teachers and remain calm. This is only a drill."

At the five minute mark, the school alarm system went off with measured siren blasts echoing through the halls. We lined up at our classroom door and were led into the gym. Sitting on the floor in groups, we were told not to make a sound. Then custodial staff chained the doors closed, and overhead lights were turned off. Several girls screamed in the dark until a few teachers turned on flashlights. Principal Evans held a flashlight, illuminating his face and told everyone it was imperative to keep silent. We sat in near darkness for five minutes then were released back to our classrooms.

It was hard to think about anything else for the rest of the day. It was clear to me, that the citizens of Cedarville, including Principal Evans, believed themselves to be under attack. We were told to stay together in groups and not to go out at night unless accompanied by an adult. Everyone was taking it seriously, except for Joel. He rolled his eyes in the hall as girls huddled together, wondering if they could defend themselves against "Frogman" with their spiral notebooks. "I can't believe any of this," Joel shook his head. "The Police Department and the Texas Rangers believe we are being stalked by an unknown predator and I have just been outed by Dr. Simon Tattinger of Washington State as a juvenile prankster. How could he think this is all a hoax?!" Joel crumbled to the floor under his locker.

Now I knew why Joel looked and smelled like rotted broccoli mixed with curdled milk. His pen pal believed him to be a hoaxer. But that wasn't all, his favorite biologist at the New York Museum of Natural History was siding with Dr. Tattinger. While the local police thought there was an unknown creature roaming the hills of Cedarville, the only opinions Joel cared about were those of the biologists and zoologists. To make matters worse, Soren Bergman agreed that Joel could be faking information about a new undocumented creature on his website. Joel was miserable, but there was one other person at school that might have been having a worse day.

Coach McGrath limped through the halls, taping up photocopied pictures of a silver whistle on a blue cord. The picture of the random whistle looked like he just copied it off of some athletic store website. He offered fifty dollars for its safe return and gave a 'no questions asked' policy. He also listed the whistle's accomplishments at the bottom of the page. The missing whistle had made it to the play-offs seven times and won regionals six times, and this was just for football. It was his lucky whistle and no substitute would ever do; not even the new whistle given to him by one of the parents.

During the seventh-grade football game last night in which they lost badly, Coach McGrath tripped walking into the locker room at half-time. He didn't catch himself because one hand held his clip board and the other had his stapled thumb wrapped in a bandage. He collided with the floor, chipping his front tooth.

Now he was in the hall, wrestling with a tape dispenser and posting his flyers all over the school grounds. When school let out, he once again stood by the front doors as we loaded onto the buses. He handed out flyers to each and every student. No one got by him, I mean, no one.

"I have one already sir," I said as politely as I could, trying not to stare at the gap in his smile.

"Then take another one and be sure to share it with your friends. Remember I'm offering a fifty dollar reward." He then handed me five more flyers. "Pass them out on the bus, give them to your neighbors. You never know."

The same teachers were stationed in the same positions outside by the buses, keeping a dutiful watch as they monitored the school grounds for any breach of an undiscovered beast. Coach McGrath was clearly not interested in any monster invasion of our school. If a scary creature had showed up to our school, Coach would have given him fifty flyers about his whistle and asked it to "spread the word" with its scary creature friends.

The floor of the bus was littered with flyers. I felt kind of bad for him. He seemed so desperate to get that whistle back. Looking out the window as we were heading home on the bus, I could see that the Coach's whistle wasn't the only thing missing in town. Tethered to trees and taped to street signs were pictures of a white missing dog, named Molly. There was a five hundred dollar reward for her safe return. The neighborhood watch had also cluttered Cedarville with my blurry, blobby photo. I counted 42 flyers of the Frogman Monster in the ten miles between school and my house.

"Wow. Those pictures are really terrible. They should have just paid me for one of mine. You can't even tell what "IT" is…." Joel smirked.

"Yeah, too bad for them… It's just a big dark blob." My throat tightened and I felt sweaty even though I knew I was unrecognizable in the photos. I coughed trying to clear my throat, but it didn't help; rising up from inside me was a small fragment of doubt. What if someone did recognize me?

It was a quick turn around once I was home. I barely had enough time to change clothes and make it to basketball practice on time. Here's what you need to know. Dad took me to practice again. He carried a heavy flashlight. So embarrassing. I guess he thinks that "I" am afraid of bright light. We walked into the gym and that's when I learned that CJ was part of our team. CJ was the new volunteer for all demonstrations, from tying shoes to dribbling figure eights. Even though Artie loathed being in the spotlight, he despised that CJ was now his father's 'go-to' team member. This put Artie into a horrible mood. All weekend long, Joel and Artie sulked and stewed.

"There's no way CJ is a kid. He's an android sent from the future to ruin my life." Artie sulked while we Zyped each other. If you're wondering why we are Zyping it's because we are not allowed out of the house, due to the fact that they think we are under attack.

Joel countered with, "I agree that he is not a twelve-year old student. The android from the future is an interesting twist. But I am still leaning toward CJ being a community college drop-out and that we were all being punked for a new reality television show. Most likely Principal Evans and Coach McGrath are in on the TV series secret. Hopefully, they will only shoot 22 episodes and then CJ will be on his way. Better yet, CJ's TV show will be cancelled before it ever airs. That would be fantastic!"

I had to agree that CJ was more of a problem than Dirk ever was. My weekend was unfortunately all about my mom's strategic campaign against Frogman—in other words, me! Her arsenal of weapons included copied pages of my blurry photo, duct tape, and each and every citizen arming them-selves with a heavy duty flashlight, umbrella, or walk-ing stick. My mom secretly carried a doughnut in her purse in case of attack. That way, in case the monster forgot to eat breakfast, she could feed it while running to safety. She reasoned it might not be so dangerous if it had a full stomach.

After dinner, Mom was glued to the television. An earlier press conference replayed on the news. It was the elderly lady whose dog Molly was missing. "Please if you have any information regarding my poor, poor Molly, please call me at 555-4289. I know she must be very afraid. She's eleven years old, blind in one eye, likes to eat cheese and hates the color beige. I'm offering a five hundred dollar reward for her safe return. She was last seen pooping in my yard. Please help."

Mom and Dad had tears in their eyes. "That poor woman is just suffering so…" my mom sniffled. "Molly's probably like a child to her. I do hope someone finds her and soon. It's not good for an elderly person to be under such stress."

The next day there were new pet flyers posted along our street and placed on our doorstep. One was of a missing cat, a tabby named Oliver. This cat lives in the neighborhood next to us and has been missing several days. That night there was a new press conference on our local news. Mr. Hughes reached out to the community for help in finding his beloved cat; the same missing cat from my neighborhood. Mr. Hughes snuffled a tear then spoke in a calm, even tone. "Oliver is a two year old, rescue cat. He likes trees, sunshine, and hates rain. Sure, he has disappeared before, but that was only for a few hours. Oliver has now been missing almost a week. Something is terribly wrong. Oliver loves watching Jeopardy and has never missed an episode of Nightline until now. Please help!"

At church the next morning, Nate was overwhelmed with prayer requests for everyone's pet's safety. We spent much of the time discussing what animal makes the best pet and if Noah had any extra pets on the ark. CJ was also there. Artie didn't say a word all through church. He looked completely miserable. Our pastor prayed for everyone's safety and for the safety of Cedarville. Even he thought something awful was roaming our woods.

Chapter Sixteen

Sunday night was pretty much the same. There was another press conference on our local news. Two families stood inside the Cedarville courthouse. One of the families, the Garcias, live in my subdivision. The Garcias were missing a small, mixed mutt named Bear. Mr. Garcia stood before the microphone, holding a notecard and a picture of his dog. He wiped away a tear with the cuff of his sleeve and began, "Bear is fluffy and sweet. He hates cats and all small animals. He likes to chew on a bone and despises dry dog food. He also hates being brushed or bathed. We miss him so much. Please help us find him. Thank you."

The Johnson's then came forward with a picture of their missing cat, Millie. The Johnson's teenage daughter, Bree, stepped to the microphone holding a picture of her cat. "Hi, I'm Bree and my cat, Millie, has been missing all afternoon. She's a white long hair, who likes naps, butterflies, birds, and goldfish. Her favorite color is aquamarine." Bree stammered for a second then wiped a tear from her cheek before continuing on, "Oh, yeah...She also does not answer to her name. She will come to you if you offer her a vanilla latte. Please help. Thank you!"

Monday morning there was no more room left on the street sign at the end of my road, nor on the chain link fence that surrounded our community swimming pool. Flyers with missing animals covered the metal fence and posts. Everyone on the bus talked about their pets and how they all had to poop indoors. A few girls sobbed over all the poor animals that were missing. It was not a fun start to my day, at all.

Joel rearranged his books in his locker when I walked up. "How was your weekend?" I was afraid to know, but it couldn't be worse than mine or Artie's.

"Oh, it was great if you like to be called a hoaxer in front of the known universe. I obviously have to say, known universe, because to imply that we definitely know everything about outer space without factual, verifiable data to back that up would be purely speculative, possibly egregious on my part, bordering on erroneous."

I was wrong, I mean really wrong. Joel had a worse weekend. Whenever he is super upset he starts to talk like a dad.

"Basically, everyone I have ever looked up too, my pen pals and these great professors and scientists, think that somehow I have been able to fake the footprints and photographs. They think I made these images with computerized special effects. I can't believe it!" Joel fumed.

Artie tried to lift Joel's spirits, "The Police think it's real. The Texas Rangers and the Texas Parks and Wildlife Department believe there really is something out there. They take you seriously."

"They don't count. They are not scientists. They are not writing journal articles and changing our understanding about life on this planet. Who cares what they think? Besides they are jumping ahead and drawing conclusions on an animal that we don't know enough about at this point. It's very unprofessional and negligent. Because of their incompetence, I can't go to the pond or anywhere else in the woods and continue my investigation. I can't gather more evidence to prove I'm not a phony!"

Unfortunately, at this moment CJ walked by. Artie and I reached out and took Joel by his arms. I didn't want to see him in detention because he challenged CJ to a duel, like on his favorite TV show. "Okay, all right... I'm fine!" Joel broke loose from our grip. At that moment, CJ turned back and smirked at the three of us.

"That's it! He's going down. I may not be able to gather information on Frogman, but I can prove that CJ Dillon is a liar and a fake."

"Super. That's super..." Artie didn't know which was worse, that I was Frogman or that Joel was taking on a bigger blockhead than Dirk the jerk. Dirk wasn't having a good Monday either. His social studies homework was missing again. He had to rewrite his paper before school let out or else he wouldn't be able to quarterback tomorrow night. He was in a foul mood all morning. Coach McGrath was not in a better mood either. His lucky whistle was still missing, and on his way to school Monday morning, his car got a flat tire. After he changed his tire, he promptly attacked all of his flyers with a magic marker, crossing out the fifty dollar reward and doubling it to an even hundred.

Coach McGrath had the attention of all students and staff. In between and during classes, students and teachers rummaged through trash bins, checked under tables, and rifled through their belongings. Teachers questioned students, and several staff members from the front office interviewed Coach as to where he last saw his whistle. I could see he was getting desperate as he stuffed four pieces of gum into his mouth all at once. His jaw worked over that gum the entire day.

Coach McGrath's whistle was still missing the next day. Since the inside of the school had been searched the previous day, students and teachers now looked out the windows searching the school grounds from the safety of the classrooms. Scouring the grounds from the windows was useless. No one had binoculars and the whistle didn't have a locator beacon of light that pulsed every three seconds that could be seen five miles away. The lucky whistle remained lost. The new rumor around school was that Frogman had taken Coach's whistle, and most likely would return it to collect the hundred dollar reward.

Dirk managed to rewrite his homework. He turned it in to the teacher on time so he could be the starting quarterback for the league's game tonight. Dirk looked cool and confident all day long, even when his library book went missing. Someone was definitely messing with him.

After school, I came home to discover that my mom was hosting another Neighborhood Watch meeting. Since Jackie Dillon would be at the football game tonight, there would be a very special guest to speak in her place. While Libby and I helped put extra chairs in the living room, the phone rang. Mom answered it in the kitchen. It was Grandma Alice. She was calling from Florida, her favorite vacation spot. But at this moment she was not enjoying the sunshine or the beach. In fact, Grandma Alice was very distraught. I could hear Mom on the phone in the kitchen, "Oh, dear. OH DEAR. OH, MYYYY!"

Grandma Alice had received a very disturbing phone call from her sister Edith, who lives in Pittsburgh. It seemed that Aunt Edith nearly died. Aunt Edith had been watching the nightly news while eating pasta when she almost choked on a meatball.

"Choked! Choked!!" Grandma Alice wailed, "Edith was so frightened she nearly kicked the bucket over a plate of spaghetti! Huge frogs are eating people's pets? What in the world is going on over there?" Grandma Alice then proceeded to tell Mom how our small town was featured on the nightly news in Pittsburgh. After Mom reassured Grandma that we were not being invaded, she hung up the phone and welcomed into our home members of our local monster awareness club.

Once the members of the neighborhood club arrived, they gathered around the television to watch the evening news. There was another press conference held in front of our courthouse. Mason Clark, age seven, stood on a chair in front of a podium. "This morning, my hamster Gizmo was in his cage in my room when I fed him breakfast. He ate celery. I went to school and when I came home, Gizmo was gone. Also, I can't find my remote control to my video games." Then with a bit of prodding from his mother, Mason continued, "Please help me find Gizmo. He's small, brown, and doesn't like his cage. He gets out of his cage A LOT. I think Frogman came and took him and my remote control." Mason started crying. His mother helped him down off the chair and hugged him as one of our town's librarians moved the chair out of her way and smiled in front of the many reporters and concerned citizens who had showed up for this press conference.

"Hello, I'm Lydia Fisher from Cedarville Free Public Library. I would just like to remind everyone that we have a wonderful selection of books that can be checked out for two whole weeks since we are encouraged to stay indoors at this time. I can't think of a better way to spend time with family and friends than reading a good book together. Also, I would like to point out that we have a wonderful selection of books on various monsters, myths, and legends. From the Loch Ness Monster to Werewolves, I think you'll find we have all your monsters covered. We're open every day from 9 a.m. until 9 p.m. except for Sunday. Thank you and see you soon!"

Police Chief Bob Carlton approached the podium. He was not smiling. In fact, he looked like he had just found a toenail in his coffee. He cleared his throat, adjusted the microphone and began, "Citizens of Cedarville, I am here to inform you that next week, over the Thanksgiving holiday, local law enforcement plus police from surrounding communities, Texas Parks and Wildlife, and the Texas National Guard will be participating in a hunt for the beast that has become known locally as "Frogman." We will search public parks and public areas. Citizens with privately owned lands will be contacted for possible search sites as well. The hunt will begin Wednesday evening and will continue until Saturday evening. Each participant will be wearing an orange vest with an orange arm band with the state seal on it. Please use caution when out and about this Thanksgiving. Be aware of your surroundings and please be mindful of the many men and women who have volunteered to help hunt this creature. We are here to capture this specimen alive. We are asking the general population to stay out of these areas during those days. Thank you for your help. Our office will keep everyone posted as new information comes in. Thank you."

I couldn't move. I was stunned. They were bringing in the Texas National Guard to hunt -me! I was scared but then I realized I was going to be alright. Unless they were going door to door with a big tub of mud to smear on children of my size, I was fine. Besides, Joel hadn't recognized me yet, and hopefully never will. All I have to do is hide who I am from him for the rest of my life or at least until I grad-uate high school and go to college. Most likely Joel will never throw buckets of mud at me so I should be fine. I breathed a sigh of relief in my living room full of monster hunters.

Dad turned off the television and Mom announced that she had a special guest who had found time in his schedule to answer questions and speak about Frogman. The doorbell rang and in walked Joel and his mom.

Joel was tonight's special guest. Everyone clapped enthusiastically as he stepped in front of the fireplace facing the members of the Neighborhood Watch. I clapped unenthusiastically. I walked to the back of the living room wondering if he brought sacks of dirt with him. Instead, he carried a small laptop computer and my dad opened up a projection screen. In five minutes we were all staring at a picture of me in mid-jump. The picture was dark and a bit blurry, but I could easily see Piper's hair, her shoulder and arm. I, on the other hand, was mostly a blob, but I could still see that it was me under the caked-on mud that was flaking off in spots.

Joel began with, "So here is the back of Piper's head, left shoulder and part of her left arm. It is quite clear that she is being held by the creature over his shoulder, if that is what we can call it for now, as he was in mid-jump. They landed in the tree-line near the pond. You can make out a little bit of the creature's arm and wrist as he is holding her. Of course, I am not suggesting we know that it is a 'he.' But until further investigation I will refer to the creature as "Frogman." "You mean, a monster?" A woman shuddered sitting on a couch.

"Well, ma'am, I'm not calling it a monster as of yet. We don't know enough. Is this a living, breathing, creature? Absolutely. Is it a phantom of some kind? Most likely not. Here's what we know... It made footprints in the dirt. Things that are real, animals that are real, leave footprints. If you are in the woods and you see a deer track you know that a deer has recently walked by that way. Deer tracks equals deer, just like coyote tracks equal a real, live coyote. The footprints I cast were found near a water source."

Joel told the adults how important water is to animals for them to live when all I could think about was he had more than one of my footprints. I had only known about and seen one copy. Now he told the Neighborhood Watch that there is more than one. This must be the new evidence he was going to share with Soren Bergman and Beast T.V. I was now worried how good the track print was. I felt the air in the room become hot. I felt sweaty and dizzy. Joel kept on talking.

"The water source is in the woods with an ample food supply." Joel reiterated.

"Well, of course it has a great food supply. It's jumping through our community eating our pets. When it runs out of pets, we'll be next! It's a miracle that Dirk and Piper survived, God help us all!" Mrs. Langford, our neighbor said, clasping her hands together. I couldn't believe what I was hearing. Mrs. Langford has known me all of my life. I would never eat her dog, much less Dirk or Piper. My head was still spinning and now my stomach churned with these gross thoughts. I sat down on the floor to hear the rest of Joel's presentation.

"We don't know what is eating our pets and if they are actually being eaten or are just lost. Pets have gone missing well before Frogman came to our area. If this thing is amphibian, most likely it is in hibernation mode. It could easily have found a den near a water source and is sleeping through the winter. It hasn't been seen since Halloween night. It could have left our area."

"Wherever it is...it must be stopped. That in the photo... does not look harmless," A woman interjected.

"We don't have enough information yet. How do we know it wasn't saving Dirk and Piper? Isn't that what we all thought in the beginning?" Joel asked. "Besides, I just got word from my inside source at the Police Station that Millie the cat was found hiding in the pantry eating goldfish crackers. And tomorrow we'll probably hear that Mason's mother has found his remote control under a couch. I don't think Frogman is breaking into homes and taking the remote control to video games. But to be safe, I wouldn't leave your pets outside. I do think this creature is of an amphibian nature. I found toe pads on one of my footprints that I cast. Frogs are not discerning when it comes to food. If they can fit it into their mouth, they're going to try to eat it."

They were several "gasps" and a few "yucks" as Joel continued on, "Take care to notice your surroundings, watch your pets and children and probably the elderly too, because there is going to be a huge hunt starting next week. I think it best to stay out of their way and out of the woods. I do not agree with Police Chief Carlton. I do not think this is a malevolent animal. But to be safe, until more is known, know where your children and pets are. Thank you."

My father followed after Joel, repeating the information from tonight's press conference on the news. He even included the bit about the library. As the Neighborhood Watch dispersed for the evening, Mom gave each member an organic pepper spray key chain.

Windows and doors were checked twice by Mom and Dad to make sure they were bolted, locked and latched before we all went to bed. Mom was not convinced that Mason had misplaced his hamster. She was truly worried. Libby was so scared that she slept with her light on as she had been doing for several nights. She was also upset that the monster had not been caught since it was interrupting her time after school to hang out with her friends. Sam, of course, just giggled whenever he heard my parents discussing the strange goings on in town.

I had my own concerns, like... if I can't walk to the end of my driveway without adult supervision, how in the world would I be able to ride my bike to Wilson's Pet Store and buy a bag of crickets? I was starving for insects. It had been days since I ate a bug. Now that it was nearly the end of November, bugs were just nowhere to be found. And what about this other footprint cast? Was Joel going to line everyone up in town and try to match it to our feet like that Princess and the glass slipper? I was hungry and worried when Artie called asking how the meeting went.

"Hey, Joel just called and told me how he was the special guest at your mom's meeting tonight."

"Yeah."

"So, how did he do? Have they figured out that they're actually meeting in the monster's lair; that they're sitting inches from him on the couch and sharing a bowl of Cheezy Squares Party Mix?" Artie was laughing to himself.

"Uhmmm, no. I really think this has gone too far. We can't go outside. Our school seems to be on lockdown most of the time. Pets are missing and they are blaming me."

"They're not blaming you. They are blaming the monster." Artie stopped laughing.

"Then why does it feel like they are blaming me? Why are they so scared? It's just me."

"But they don't know that. It's going to be ok. Remember don't do anything and they will think the monster has moved on. Everything will go back to normal."

"What if it doesn't?"

"It will. Just don't do anything."

"No, I mean, what if it's not normal. I am Frogman. What if I am becoming a real, live monster and this is just the beginning?"

"Alex, I never once thought you ate one of those missing cats. You've never really been a cat person."

"True...but now I am just so hungry and there's no more insects. Mom won't let me out of her sight to get crickets at the pet store, and that's because she's scared of me, only she doesn't know it's me. It's become too complicated."

I went to bed that night wondering if maybe I wasn't so good. Maybe I was becoming something else. Maybe there was something to what those women in the Neighborhood Watch were saying about me, and I just hadn't noticed it yet.

At two in the morning I awoke to a dog barking on our street. I rolled over thinking it would quiet down but the barking actually got louder as it came closer to my house. I peeked out the living room window and there was the Garcia's missing dog, Bear, in the Langford's yard yapping up at a tree. I thought about what Artie had said about doing nothing. I tried to go back to sleep but then I thought about Bear being hungry and cold and his family missing him. I quietly opened the front door and jumped over to Bear, snatching him up in my arms before he had a chance to run away.

Bear does not like hugs. He also doesn't like heights. I know this to be true since Bear struggled in my arms, scratched at my chest, and snapped at my chin. Knowing that the Garcia's live in my neighborhood, I jumped three blocks over and landed on Pecan Ridge Road. I quickly checked the address on Bear's collar as he twisted in my arms and bit at my hand. I found the right house and quietly jumped into their back yard. Luckily, Bear's residence had a doggie door that led into the house. Bear sniffed around his yard, turned and growled at me, then disappeared through his door.

Three days would pass before I discovered that I put Bear in the wrong back yard. I was off by one house. Bear made himself comfortable during the night by eating parts of the living room sofa and chairs. In the paper, the police reported the house was strewn with pillow stuffing. Never had they seen furniture murdered by such a little mutt. However, the police believed it to be a miracle since Bear was still alive after digesting part of a shoe, a piece of carpeting, and half of a house plant. It was also reported the family believed that Bear had been traumatized by Frogman and went berserk. To sum it all up...I need to take Artie's advice and lay low.

Chapter Seventeen

The Wednesday morning before Thanksgiving, Mom woke us all up and gave us a list of chores to do. Super. So glad I am not at school... Libby dragged the vacuum cleaner behind her as she wandered around the house half-asleep, eating a bran muffin. As the crumbs fell to the floor, she trampled them into the carpet. Within another step, the vacuum cleaner was sucking up her muffin mess. This, I have to say, is one of the few times that Libby has had a good idea. For his part, Sam promised to keep his toys in his room and used a feather duster to clean the furniture he was able to reach. What tasks was I given to do you may ask? I cleaned out all the trash cans, cleaned the bathrooms, including toilets, and washed windows from the inside. Yeah, this seems fair.

Mom was at the health food store where anything that tastes good, is banned from their shelves and freezers. I was expecting the typical Tofurkey this year when Mom arrived back home and asked me to bring in the grocery bags. That's when I saw it. There it was in the most beautiful, plastic casing I have ever seen; a real turkey. It had been years since we had a real turkey for Thanksgiving. I could not wait for tomorrow!

Thanksgiving morning I was in the kitchen peeling potatoes. A bucket of potatoes. I didn't mind though. For once, I was more excited about eating real food than a grasshopper.

In the dining room Sam tried to fold napkins while Libby set the table. Mom checked the turkey, mixed the stuffing, and steamed green beans. She was a flurry of arms, hands, and slotted spoons. It was then that I noticed that there were four extra place settings at the table. Now I realized why I was peeling a bucket full of potatoes, why we were having a real turkey for Thanksgiving. The doorbell rang. Mom put the turkey on the table and went to the door.

My house was breached once more. We hadn't started eating yet, and this was already the worst Thanksgiving ever, including the time that Mom prepared okra and tomato salad with kale chips for dessert. I sat across from CJ not feeling thankful at all. Katie sat next to Sam. Big mistake. Doesn't Mom remember our field trip to the football game and how Katie made Sam cry all night? The worst part was that CJ had an older brother. Ryker sat directly across from Libby and by the way she acted, I could see she thought he was good looking. She even swallowed her gum rather than put her slobbery, spit-filled wad on the edge of her plate for after dinner chewing enjoyment. Ryker was just a taller and more muscular version of CJ, except he had brown hair. Jackie sat at the other end of the table with my parents.

Mom gave Dad "the look" and that's when he cleared his throat and said a Thanksgiving prayer. It was during Dad's prayer I offered up my own. I told God it wasn't worth eating a real turkey if I had to share it with CJ. While everyone had their eyes closed, I opened one of mine to see that CJ, Ryker, and Katie were staring at the rest of us. That's when Katie burst into a fit of giggles. The glasses, silverware, and plates began clanging and rattling against the table. CJ and Ryker tried to kick Katie underneath the table but hit the table leg and each other. At the other end of the table, their mother gave them all a murderous glare. My mom, squinched her eyes tightly closed, and sat as still as if she were covered in scorpions.

By the time my dad finished his prayer with a resounding "Amen!," he was the only one left with a bowed head and closed eyes. We all watched CJ, Ryker, and Katie try to muffle their laughter. Jackie scowled so hard at her children I thought she would arrest them and take them to jail. Yet, my mom, tried to act like nothing weird, or inappropriate had happened. As Dad cut into the turkey, Mom began doing what she does when she's nervous. She began blabbering away.

"Umm, you know, our family has this really sweet tradition," Mom started.

"Oh, Noooooooooooooo," was all I could think. I wanted to run away. Why couldn't my super power be teleportation. I would give almost anything to be anywhere else, including shopping at the mall with Libby and her stupid friends.

"So... what we like to do," Mom continued, without any notice to the panic and fear etched into Libby's and my face, "is go around the table and say one thing that you are thankful for this past year. It's a super special tradition that our children look forward to every year." Then Mom looked at our faces, overlooking the horror in our eyes, and gave a gooey, "Awwwww."

"Alex, dear, why don't you start and show them what I mean." Mom smiled as Dad continued carving up the turkey. I knew what Mom meant; she wanted to hear how thankful I was for our family, new friends, Mom's internet seed business, and Grandma's new knee. Looking across the table at CJ, I did not feel very thankful at all. There was only one thing that came to mind so I said it, to my mother's embarrassment. "I am thankful for turkey." I could not have predicted the chain of events that followed. Sam was thankful for Frogman, which made everyone gasp. Katie was thankful for cupcakes. Libby was thankful for gum and her computer. Ryker was thankful for pizza and then it was CJ's turn. He looked up and down the table first.

"Hmmm, that's kinda hard. Let me think for a second. He opened his mouth to speak, and suddenly with the force of hurricane winds sneezed all over the turkey as Dad placed the platter of mantastic meat in the center of the table.

I had been hit, but I wasn't the only one; so had Sam, Libby, Katie and my dad! It was a slimy assault of germs of undebatable origin! Droplets, blobs, and globules of disgusting CJ DNA had splattered and sprayed across the turkey!!!

No one moved. Not one inch. Dad froze where he was standing, leaning over the table. Mom gasped at her now contaminated Thanksgiving dinner. Without a word, Mom took the platter of turkey and carried it to the kitchen. She came back to the table with a clenched smile that looked as if it had been applied to her face with Sooper Dooper glue. "I have an idea. In keeping with the Thanksgiving spirit, why don't we follow Ryker's lead and order pizza this year? Great idea. Super! Just super!" Within seconds, Mom had cleared the table and was on the phone with Pizza Palace.

I looked into the kitchen where Mom was on her cell phone and dumping the turkey in the trash. Then one by one, she dumped the stuffing, mashed potatoes, and gravy into the trash too. I was fuming. It had been years since I was able to enjoy a traditional Thanksgiving meal that wasn't made of cauliflower, pumpkin seeds, and tofu. CJ had his napkin over his mouth trying to hide his laughter, even though his bouncing shoulders gave him away. I wanted to kick him through the dining room wall.

Mom returned to the table and said with a grim face, "Pizza Palace is out of pizza; every kind of pizza, including anchovies and olives. I don't understand it. How do you run out of pizza on Thanksgiving? So... give me a few minutes and I will whip something up just as good. I make a terrific asparagus and quinoa casserole. Jackie, would you like to help me in the kitchen?"

CJ stopped laughing. In fact, he now looked scared. Katie immediately asked Libby what asparagus was. She looked confused as she saw the frightened looks that CJ and Ryker were giving each other.

Jackie stood up, gave her kids one last long look that threatened immediate death if they moved a muscle. Libby and I washed the dishes by hand and reset the table. Then after another hour and a half we sat down to a table with fake mashed potatoes made with cauliflower. Jackie and Libby followed Mom with kale chips, broccoli salad, and the infamous casserole. There's no way the pilgrims would have been thankful for this meal. However, Mom did get her own style of revenge. She put heaping mounds of all the gross vegetables on CJ's plate. "This food is so good for you. It's called eating clean and it's full of vitamins and minerals. I grew these from my own seeds too! Eat up!"

CJ started to sweat. Katie was on the verge of crying. Ryker held his breath and gobbled down what he could. They were all scared; really terrified of Mom's cooking. It was the only good thing that happened all day. Halfway through dinner, my day continued to improve. Jackie received an urgent phone call on her cell. It was the police station and they needed her to come in for a quick press conference.

Jackie told her kids to hustle to the car as fast as they could and put Ryker in charge of the other two. She thanked Mom and Dad over and over again for the fantastic Thanksgiving meal. Since they couldn't stay for dessert, that meant more pumpkin pie for me.

After dessert, Dad turned on the news. The press conference had already begun. Police Chief Carlton stood behind a podium with ten microphones from various news outlets. One microphone had the GNN logo on it. A reporter from Global News Network was in town. Another microphone had CNC on it. That's Central News Corporation. They are the second biggest national news network. Then there was Selfie Celebrity Magazine. I couldn't believe it! The number one celebrity magazine that covers movies, television shows, and of course, celebrity selfies. Why in the world did they send a reporter to our small town of Cedarville? It's supposed to be a monster, not a movie star.

Police Chief Carlton sported a new haircut and with too much hair gel. "Again, I would like to remind the public to please be aware of your surroundings and stay out of wooded areas and parks until Saturday evening. Traps have been set and the hunt is on. If you see Toasty tarts, pizza, cooked turkeys, candy bars, and hamburgers in trees and bushes, please do not go near them, do not eat them. I repeat, do not eat them. We are trying to bait the creature. Thank you for your cooperation." He repeated the monster hotline number and stepped away as Jackie Dillon walked up to the podium. She answered questions from the crowd of reporters.

"No, we do not believe it is an elephant crossed with a kangaroo. No, I have not seen the latest Hogzilla movie. I doubt it is Hogzilla. Yes, I do like the movie Galaxy Wars." The questions kept coming. "'Monster' is a relative term. But, yes, it is positively a monster! It most likely is an undocumented creature, yes, absolutely. I think we should be responsible and consider that this creature is dangerous. 'Do dragons exist?' I am not a dragon expert, but no. 'Could this be a dragon?' Sure." The crowd of reporters gasped. "'Is the Loch Ness Monster technically a dragon?' That's a good question. I think this concludes our press conference. Thank you and good night."

The phone rang immediately. It was Joel and he was fuming. "I can't believe they are baiting traps with Canadian bacon and pineapple pizza. Are these people nuts? Do they think that this Frogman actually orders pizza from Pizza Palace and has it delivered out to the pond?"

Joel was being sarcastic of course, but I thought this was pure genius. Would Pizza Palace deliver to the pond? If so, I could just add my own special toppings of dragonflies on top of all that gooey cheese and pepperoni. My little daydream was interrupted by Joel's continued ranting. "As if this creature is going to want to eat hot dogs with mustard and relish," Joel bristled. "This animal eats what it finds in the woods. Chocolate cupcakes do not grow on bushes. Tater Tots do not lie on the ground under trees as if they are fallen acorns. Pot roasts do not hang from trees either. I have no idea what these hunters are thinking, except that they believe it's the kind of monster that likes to eat at Big Bart's All You Can Eat Buffet. What they are going to do is make this amphibian sick."

"So you still think this monster is an amphibian?"

"Yes. I am convinced of it. I don't think it's a monster either. It's just an animal. But who listens to me anyway?"

Joel hung up the phone and I went to bed listening to my mother lock and relock all the doors and windows. She left the porch light on all night, too. Mom and Dad came and checked on all of us before bed. Mom tried to act nonchalant as she opened my closet door to make sure that no horrific beast was trying on my shirts. Satisfied that the house was monster-free, they went to bed.

Chapter Eighteen

The next morning Dad woke us up early to help Mom with the annual Historical Society's set up of the manger scene on our court house lawn. Driving over to the Historical Society's storage locker I couldn't help but notice that the skies were filled with birds: All kinds of birds. Mom stared up into the sky and Dad had a hard time keeping his eyes on the road.

"What in the world?" Mom squinched her eyes and leaned forward in her seat to get a better look out of` the front window of our car. "I've never seen so many birds before. It's kind of creepy." She turned around to look back at us kids to make sure we hadn't flown away. "Seatbelts all on? Good." She smiled as she checked that our windows were rolled up.

"I've never seen anything like this—ever. There's turkey buzzards, crows, hawks, all flying together. There's so many! What could be going on?" Dad slowed down the car as we stared out of the windows at the dark, swirling mass of birds that circled the skies like a slow moving tornado.

"It's like a scene out of a horror movie, or a plague from the Bible," Mom said locking everyone's doors. "Everyone's window rolled up all the way? You know you can't be too safe."

We mumbled that our windows were closed. Sam pointed at a huge turkey buzzard that sat atop the sign for our Emergency Medical Clinic. It was as if that ugliest of birds waited to pick off any one who didn't recover from a sprained ankle or cold sore. I know my mom can be really weird and overly protective, but it was beginning to freak me out.

As we turned past two gas stations, there in the parking lot of a laundromat were three hawks sharing a pepperoni pizza. Crows worked over donuts that hung from trees that lined our streets. Buzzards picked at a meatloaf in front of our Post Office. The baiting had worked, just not as expected. Every scavenger bird in the whole state had invaded our town.

A police car met us at the Historical Society's storage unit at the request of my mom. She demanded assistance to make sure the volunteers remained safe as we dug out an ancient sixteen piece Christmas manger set. I believe it may have been carved by someone who was at the actual event. It's that old. It was carved by one of our founding pioneers from the cedar trees that grow in our area, which is how our community got its name of Cedarville. It's also nearly life-sized and extremely heavy.

While the police officer sipped coffee and watched for monsters, we loaded up two trucks with the manger set and drove to the court house. Out on the lawn and under the protection of the same officer still sipping the same cup of coffee, Mom directed the arrangement of the manger set. This is unnecessary though since all pieces are set on the same spot on the court house lawn each and every year.

I couldn't help but notice two more news station vans while we unloaded the trucks. One was from Houston and the other from New Orleans. Reporters were out on the streets interviewing citizens that were brave enough to go outside. It shouldn't have been that scary since our sidewalks were crawling with police and national guardsmen. Our mayor walked out to see our progress. He seemed a bit jumpy as he looked around before walking the twenty-five steps to where we worked. Even he was escorted by a State Trooper.

With the downtown area of Cedarville protected by officers and guardsmen, I should have felt safe. Instead, my heart was racing. I grabbed a shovel off the truck and lugged it around. It was my only weapon against these birds. I tried my best to resist the urge to jump home. I kept thinking how I can't let people, including my mom, know I'm

Frogman. On top of that, I would expose myself to all these meat-eating birds that I'm one ginormous frog that they could chow on alongside a plate of nachos. Yep, that's right. Someone put a plate of cheesy nachos in the hand of a statue of our first mayor, Lerner Falsted, that stands near the court house entrance.

The birds swarmed overhead while we worked faster than we ever had before. I grew more and more nervous. As I shifted the baby lamb around, I kept a tight grip on the shovel, just in case the birds discovered my secret.

"Are you all right?" Mom asked while I tried to push the lamb into its spot with my foot. It didn't work too well. "Use your hands. That's never going to work. And put down the shovel." She stared at me until I laid the shovel down. But as soon as the lamb was in place, I grabbed the shovel again. Mom carefully set baby Jesus in His manger. Baby Jesus is the last piece to be installed. He is positioned directly under the star. The star is carved from wood, but thirty years ago some-one painted it gold. The other pieces are plain un-painted wood. Mom stepped back with several other ladies to take in the sight. Everything must have looked good to them, since they smiled and applauded the volunteers. Next, the lights were set in the grass to be turned on at dusk. Finally, we were finished.

We got in the car and left to return home. But first Dad wanted to get ice cream as a "thank you" for volunteering for the Historical Society's Christmas scene. We pulled in at a drive-thru ice cream shop and ordered the best ice cream in the world. At the window, Dad paid for our cones. When the girl in the window handed over our ice cream, the biggest, ugliest, and scariest bird landed on our hood. We screamed as it pecked at the windshield. The girl flung our last ice cream on the front window of our car as she slammed the drive-thru window shut. We could still hear her shrieking over Libby's screams and my own. Then that bird reached its long, feathery neck around through Dad's window and tried to get his ice cream. Dad hit the gas, the bird slid off the hood of the car, and well... all we felt was a huge bump as we veered back to the front of the shop. Not one of us looked back. Mom and Libby still screamed, but it was so hard to hear them because my heart pounded in my ears.

Dad tried to calm us all down, He reassured, "It's okay. It just wanted some ice cream. That's all. It didn't want to eat us. Settle Down! Now!! Stop screaming! I didn't kill it!!! See. Turn around. It was just a pothole that I drove over. The bird flew away!" I turned around and sure enough, no dead bird. I have to say I was kind of disappointed, because that would be one less bird I would have to worry about.

We drove home, where my siblings and I could enjoy the "great indoors" for the rest of the holiday weekend, except when we went to church. By Sunday morning, the chocolate cakes, bar-b-que brisket, and potato salad had turned our town into one great masterpiece of poop. It was modern art. And it was everywhere. Not one building or sidewalk had gone untouched by these skilled and winged artisans. Bird poo splattered against windows, on cars, parking meters, and on Jackie's shoulder as we entered the front doors of the church. She wasn't the only one who was embellished by these fowl fiends. Nate got nailed twice as he held the doors open for some little old ladies as they entered the church foyer. After church many more people were targeted, including Libby, as she dashed into the parking lot to the safety of our car.

"Man down! Man down! I've been hit! I have poo in my hair!" Libby screamed while Dad scrambled to unlock the car doors. Once inside she leaned towards Mom in the car. "Is it bad? How bad is it? Oh my gosh! This is the worst day of my life! How could this have happened?"

Chapter Nineteen

"I know exactly how this has happened," Joel fumed, over the phone. "These birds are scavengers. They are opportunists. This plan has failed! All they did was give these birds diarrhea. Do you know how much bird poop is actually out there now?"

"Uhmmm, no… no I really don't." I knew things were bad. On our way home from church, we saw State Troopers outside holding umbrellas while checking a game camera, even though there wasn't a cloud in the sky.

"Well, I will tell you. There's a lot! I mean a lot!" Our roof, driveway and back patio look like they're covered in snow. Guess who gets to scrub the patio and driveway clean? … I do! And I found a pile of puked up hotdog on my lawn too. But before I could do anything, Ranger ate it! The birds are pooping and throwing up! This city has no idea what they are doing. And if you ask me, there are more squirrels in my yard too."

"What do squirrels have to do with this?" I asked. I really didn't know.

"Just wait for it. The second wave is coming. I've got to clean the patio. I'll see you tomorrow." Joel hung up the phone and I thought about what he said. I knew bird poo wasn't the worst of our problems; even though it was bad. Mom had made our house Monster Control Central. Her cell phone buzzed all day and she neglected her internet seed business, not to mention her compost pile. She updated her white board with every new bit of information called in by friends, neighbors, and other concerned citizens.

Here's some of her list:

*Graysons Grocery is out of all meat products except for canned ham and anchovies.

*There is no peanut better left in stores in town, anywhere.

*An emergency shipment of meat is coming in sometime tomorrow at Graysons Grocery. This could be a rumor... must verify.

*The Health food store is doing record business. All organic and gluten free meats and cheeses are sold out.

*Not one locally sourced vegetable has sold all weekend even though they are on sale.

*Nothing relevant has been caught on any camera traps set in the woods.

*This morning, two raccoons were eating tortilla chips and drinking soda on the third aisle of the Quickie-Mart and Gas station. They left without paying.

And there it was... the second wave.

That last item on Mom's white board. In two hours, Mom drafted Dad, Libby and me to keep a running list of any and all sightings that came in. We had several poster boards taped to the walls of our living room.

It looked like this:

*Raccoon found eating leftover pizza in Mrs. Mayes backyard. She thinks it's a meat-lover's special with cheese inside the crust. Extra-large.

*Three raccoons spotted peeping on the Gillis family through their kitchen window while their children ate the last of their peanut butter on crackers.

*An opossum laid on the Thompson family trampoline and ate a chocolate chip granola bar. Chocolate chips or raisins. They couldn't be sure.

*Eight raccoons rummaged through trash behind the movie theatre and ate left-over popcorn. They also pooped in the parking lot.

*Confirmed sightings of orange squirrels in a park running up and down slides. Town veterinarian believes they are not a new species, but are local squirrels covered in orange cheesy chip dust.

*Seven raccoons have been spotted at the recycling center. They ate food out of the compost pile and mixed glass bottles with plastic. Shelley Douglas and Deena Pierce are trapped inside the front office. Send help!

*A ten point buck was seen jogging down the middle of Second street. It flagrantly disregarded all laws of traffic and bolted through two red lights causing cars to swerve onto the median.

*Two coyotes are on aisle nine of Grayson's Grocery Store. They're eating pancake mix and licking bottles of maple syrup. Customers have left the store but the assistant manager is trapped in the bathroom without toilet paper. Send help!

But it was the last phone call that my dad received that sent the rest of our evening into a downward tail spin of fear, anxiety, and panic. Dr. Schueller, a Communications professor, called to inform him of the terrifying experience he and his wife had endured not twenty minutes prior.

Returning home from their Thanksgiving holiday in Dallas, they had turned into their subdivision when the headlights of their car shone brightly on the most ghastly of all creatures to ever walk the earth. It was skinny, as tall as a large dog, without fur, glowing eyes, and had long fang-like teeth. It bared its fangs at the Schuellers and stood its ground. Dr. Schueller put his car in reverse, but the beast leapt across the hood of their car and darted into the backyard of an unsuspecting neighbor. All that remained was a small drop of foamy slobber on their windshield. After quick research on the internet, Dr. Schueller and his wife are convinced they had nearly been massacred by the one and only Chupacabra.

Within the hour, it was the lead story on the 11:00 news. Kelly Meadows was reporting live from the Schueller's living room. Dr. Schueller was composed and gave great detail of their terrifying experience. Mrs. Schueller was not composed. Tears streamed down her cheeks. She tried to answer Kelly Meadows questions, but only squeeks passed over her rapidly moving lips. There were no words. Nothing intelligible.

"What my wife is trying to say is," Dr. Schueller took hold of the microphone and stared straight into the camera, "we're being invaded. We need the help of the Marines. We need them to come in and regain control of our town. We're no longer safe!"

Kelly Meadows seized her microphone from the Professor's hand and stepped toward the camera.

"You heard it here first on Live Action News 12, a new monster has come to town. Back to you, Tom."

Dad grabbed the remote with the speed of thirty cheetahs with their tails on fire and changed the channel, but it was too late. We all saw the report. Even Sam showed fear for the first time. Mom leapt off the couch to begin her night time routine with a renewed sense of urgency, grabbing the fire place poker and carrying it with her as she double-checked locked doors and windows.

Dad and Mom kissed us all goodnight, then Mom gave a speech about how much she loved us and how each one of us was special. Then she went to bed taking the fire place poker with her.

Sam came into my bedroom after everyone had fallen asleep and stood next to my bed. I woke up startled to see his face inches from mine. "What is a chupa? Are you stronger than a chupa? Can you make the chupa go away?"

"Everything is going to be all right. You have nothing to worry about."

Sam sniffled and the next thing I knew he was fast asleep in bed with me. I went to bed and thought about how crazy and out of control everything had become in our town and it's all because of me. I wondered if I should ever tell my parents about my secret or if my mom would be completely afraid of me. Then I wondered if Chupacabras were real. First thing at school tomorrow morning, I would ask Joel.

Chapter Twenty

Mom was in quite a mood at breakfast. First, she scanned the street through the front windows, and then searched the backyard for intruders through the kitchen window. She really didn't care that morning if we ate a bowl of sugar for breakfast, brushed our teeth or not, or went to school in our swimsuits. She had only one thing on her mind, but was trying to hide it, poorly, I might add. Mom tried to act natural about carrying a golf club and my baseball bat to the car. In a sing-song voice she called to us as she grabbed a hammer from the tool box in the garage, "You-Hoo! Time for school Sweeties. Get in the car. It's going to be a wonderful new Monday."

Mom pulled up in front of the school to drop us off, but first called Libby and me to her window. We walked around to her side of the car and she leaned out the window and whispered so Sam couldn't hear.

"Listen, I need you two to be extra careful from now on. Always be aware of your surroundings. I don't want to scare you but these monsters could really hurt you. I mean, we really don't know much about them. Do you understand? Stay with your friends and teachers. Don't go outside. Don't try to be brave. Just go to class and I will meet you at the bus stop later. Again, don't go outside, don't do anything that will attract attention to yourselves. Ok...I love you both very much! You're two of the greatest children a mother could ever ask for." There was a tear in her eye. Libby dashed inside the school doors. She was out of breath by the time she got to her locker. I knew I needed to act a little scared, so I walked quickly after her.

Once inside the school I turned back to wave to Mom and Sam. She gave me a slight smile as she pulled away from the curb. I suppose she was relieved that Libby and I made it safely from the car to the front doors of the school and that I displayed an appropriate amount of fear. Still, as I watched her drive away, I couldn't believe how scared she really was. She really thought she might not see us again. She probably thought there was a real chance that Frogman would pass up the cafeteria pizza to eat her children. She was terrified of Frogman. Frogman was a monster in her eyes, only I am Frogman. Am I really a monster? Should she be afraid of me? Was I going to wake up one morning and really eat someone's pet? I was now, more than ever, worried about who I was and who I was becoming. Maybe I am who they say I am? Maybe they know better....

Joel was rummaging through his locker when I walked up. I could tell he was in a horrible mood because he was dropping books and throwing crumpled pieces of paper on the floor all in search of his favorite pen. This pen, by the way, has a silhouette of a bigfoot on it. "Ugh...There you are!" He put the pen in his jacket pocket and immediately started cramming his books back into his locker.

"Everything okay?" Clearly, something was bugging him.

"Okay? Okay? Really, what a question! The people in this town are losing their minds! Not only that, our town looks like it hosted the world's largest food fight— followed by the world's largest feces festival. There's nowhere in town that hasn't been hit by scat. No one is safe from falling poop either. Men, women and children are being hit. It's like a war zone. My mom heard that the sand box at Town Park is literally full of poop now. Like, there's no more sand in the box!"

I really thought Joel would pass out. I didn't see him suck in more air during his tirade. But I was wrong... He went off again like Old Faithful, the geyser in Yellowstone National Park.

"Aaaaaaaaannnnnnnnndd furthermore, CHUPACABRA! Really?!? Who in their right mind thinks there's a Chupacabra around here?"

I started to say something but was blasted back into silence.

"I don't care that he's a professor. There isn't any precedence for this creature since before the mid 1990's."

"But couldn't you say the same thing about Frogman?" I immediately regretted that remark.

"Are you really comparing these two? First of all, all the bloodwork from suspected Chupacabras have always come back as a coyote/wolf hybrid mix. The skin samples suggest a raging case of mange. Normal animals with a horrible case of mange do not look right. A raccoon with mange is nearly unrecognizable to the average citizen. Secondly, regarding Frogman, I am a trained observationist. I saw what I saw. I have footprint casts. I have photos. Professor Schueller is not trained in observation of mammalian species. He saw a mangy coyote cross the road. Period. I stake my reputation on it."

I felt certain at this point that he made up being an observationist, but I was too afraid to call him on it. Luckily, Artie joined us and witnessed Joel's meltdown. "And speaking of reputation, my invitation to speak at the New England Cryptozoological Society has been revoked. Can you believe this? These men who have been my pen pals for several years, have uninvited me to present at this spring's conference. They say that there is concern regarding my findings and that my presentation would draw negative attention to the field. To put this all bluntly, even they have labeled me a hoaxer. Just like that! Where is their proof?"

"Everyone in town thinks the monster, I mean Frogman, is real," Artie tried to cheer him up.

"Again, that doesn't matter. What matters is that my peers understand my work. Sir Colin Pickering, Dr. Trenton Walker, Dr. Diana Craig...."

"Who?" I had no idea who these people were.

"My peers! Scientists in the field. Sir Colin Pickering of the British Museum of Natural History. He unfriended me this morning on Facelook. He's not the only one either. I'm under attack!" Just as Joel reached down to pick up one of his spiral notebooks a big, smelly shoe stomped across it. It was CJ.

"Oh, I'm sorry. I didn't see you way down there." CJ laughed. "Get it? Get it" He jabbed Joel with his elbow. "Cause you're so short." Then he looked at me. "You too!" He trotted off to catch up with a few jocks in our grade who are not fans of Dirk.

Joel grabbed his notebook and book bag without taking his eyes off CJ. "He thinks he's so smart, but he just messed with the wrong sixth-grader, because I have nothing better to do than prove to Mandy, this school, and the entire universe that CJ is nothing but a phony, a huge fraud!"

Artie and I just looked at each other. We both worried about the same thing. What if Joel annoys CJ so badly that he crushes Joel to pieces? Joel is not a fighter, not even close. Artie, Joel and I have had enough wrestling matches through the years to know that. He can be mouthy when provoked, but he also will try to defend himself. It all comes down to his crazed "monkey on your back" move. He will just jump on your back and hold on until you give up. He has impressive upper body strength that no one really gives him credit for. Still, I don't think he would come close to winning against CJ in any match.

"Let this day be remembered, as the day that I began to take CJ down!" Joel exclaimed.

"Uhmmm, okay." Artie nodded his head in support of Joel's new plan.

"Yeah, okay. Got it." I agreed in hushed tones hoping Joel would get the hint and lower his voice.

"Good. However, I can't take CJ down until tomorrow. I didn't bring my research journals to school, plus all my equipment. 'Operation Fink' legitimately starts today, but research begins tomorrow—so be ready." Joel walked off leading the way. He stood a bit taller and more confident. It's funny how anger and a new project lifts his spirits.

Chapter Twenty-One

Homework was due in Mr. Jameson's class. As he gathered our papers he paused in front of Dirk's desk. Dirk rifled through his book bag, folders and binder.

"I don't understand. I had it right here. I put it in my book bag this morning." Dirk turned his book bag upside down and dumped it onto the floor in a panic. And I knew why. "If his grades dropped any lower, he would miss the last football game of the season. He had to find his homework.

The stench that came from inside that bag made everyone flinch in their seats. Except for CJ. He was unusually quiet, as he stared straight ahead, seemingly oblivious to the wafting odors of Dirk's sweaty socks and` t-shirt that smelled like moldy broccoli.

"See me after class," Mr. Jameson gave Dirk a disapproving eye. "This has become all too common with you lately."

Dirk leaned over to jam all that stinky, smelly stuff back into his bag. CJ, however, looked ahead at the front of the room with laser focused indifference. Then, after a few seconds more, CJ, quietly and quickly turned toward Dirk and smiled.

I thought Dirk would leap across the aisle and choke CJ. I really did. Instead, Dirk punched all of his belongings inside his book bag then zipped it closed. I could hardly concentrate, no one really could. We were all staring at the bleeding knuckle on Dirk's right fist as he smacked it into his left hand.

Mr. Jameson read aloud from our text book while we all followed along, reading silently to ourselves. Except for CJ. He was passing a note to Piper, and this did not go unnoticed by me or Dirk. Piper stealthily opened the folded piece of paper, took her pencil to add a few marks and quickly handed it back. CJ looked pleased, as if he just won MVP for our district.

Dirk seethed with anger and I should have been annoyed by CJ's behavior, but I was having other issues. My skin was super dry and itchy again. I rubbed my hands together and a big piece of skin rolled right off the top of my palm. I excused myself to the bathroom. In a stall, I panicked as I felt a chunk of skin pull off the back of my neck. I dropped it in the toilet. It was so gross. I took my shirt off and freaked out as bits of skin piled off the top of my body as if I had endured one of the worst sunburns on record, except, I wasn't sunburned. I was in an absolute state of shed. I looked like a big, shedding, diseased monster.

As if my day couldn't get weirder or worse, in walked Joel. I knew it was him, because I saw his Timberline boots from under the stall door. No one wears hiking boots to school but him. I stayed as still and quiet as I could but it was no use.

"Hey, get back to class as quick as you can. I'm definitely on team Dirk now. I can't wait to expose CJ." Joel then let out a loud, creepy laugh, "Mmmwwwha-hahaha!"

"Uhmmmm. Okay. Be right there." I gulped. I was so nervous to be shedding a few feet from Joel that I broke out into a flop sweat. Even my ear lobes were perspiring. I also realized I do not have nerves of steel. My beastly froggish nerves must be made of swamp water.

"Are you alright?" Joel asked washing his hands.

"Yeah, sure. Why?" Why did I ask him 'why?' I didn't want to know. Never ask a question you don't want to know the answer to.

"Because you've been in that stall a long time. I figured your mom must have made you eat brussel sprouts last night because it really stinks in here. And from where I'm standing it looks like all you're wearing are your socks. Get dressed and hurry up." Joel dashed out of the bathroom.

Just for clarification, the bathroom already stank a great deal before I even walked in. Yes, I was in my socks, trying to get through this horrible nightmare! I stayed in that stall for a few more minutes, until the grossness of it all was over. I shook my head over the toilet and flakes, like supersized dandruff in a snowstorm, swirled down into the porcelain pot. I flushed but I was overwhelmed with the need to take a bath, or rather just sit in a tub of water. Knowing that sitting in a sink while the water ran over me would be frowned upon by teachers, staff, and Principal Evans, I splashed cold water on my face and went back to class, but not before hitting up the water fountain.

Returning to class, I instantly knew I'd missed a lot. Dirk sat at the back of the classroom. From the front of the classroom I could see Dirk's jaw clenched tightly. His veins protruded out from his neck. I looked away and took my seat, having no idea how crazy this day was going to be. But what I did know was that CJ was verifiably and undoubtedly a bigger jerk than Dirk. Who knew that was even a possibility?

Basketball practice was held after school in the elementary school gym. Dirk and his two cronies, Kevin and Randy, were there as well as CJ. What is the best way to describe tonight's practice? "Keep Away from CJ." In our practice game, the ball was also kept from Artie and me. But on a good note Artie only fell 8 times. CJ sucked up to Mr. Brandt about a billion times. He complimented Mr. Brandt on his choice of shirt, shoes, watch, socks, and begged for some of his best college and NBA stories. It was sickening. Who cares what deodorant Artie's dad uses?

As Mr. Brandt drove us home, he asked Artie about his birthday plans. Artie was turning twelve on Saturday.

"I don't know. The whole town is on lock down. There's nothing to do. There aren't any good movies out. I guess go bowling, eat pizza, and play in their arcade. I don't know." Artie shrugged.

"Bowling it is! Ok. Then Joel and Alex can spend the night. Anything you want for your birthday?" Mr. Brandt was overly excited about this party as we weaved in and out of police check points, orange cones, detour signs, and the unavoidable line of national guardsmen in their jeeps. I think Mr. Brandt tried to be as normal as he could to take our minds off the fact that everyone in our town had lost their marbles.

"So what do you want...?" Mr. Brandt asked again as we watched policemen open the back doors of a cargo van. Bloodhound dogs lunged from their crates out onto the street.

"Uhmmm, to stop growing, to stop tripping over my feet, to make a basket..."

"So, you'd like a new bike?" Mr. Brandt interrupted.

"Sure. Why not?" Artie slumped in the backseat.

After dinner, Mom went through the house for the third time to make sure we were locked inside when she got a phone call from one of the ladies from the Historical Society. She listened for a minute then hung up the phone without a word. She collapsed on a chair, mouth agape when the phone rang again. This time it was our local television reporter, Kelly Meadows. The star from the manger set on the court house lawn has disappeared. Kelly Meadows wanted to know my mom's reaction to the news since she is head of the Historical Society.

"Do you believe the star has been stolen by our very own local monsters— Frogman or the Chupacabra?" Kelly inquired over the phone. "For what purposes do you believe the monster or monsters would need the star?"

My mom was still in a daze from the news. "What?!? I don't understand. How could the star go missing when there is a huge police presence in our town? Are you sure it's missing?"

"Very much so. I am standing in front of the court house now. It's gone."

I thought my mom was going to faint. She fanned herself with her hand and finished the quick interview. "I had no idea the star was missing. This has never happened before. It is just so shocking. Why would someone take it?"

"Maybe it's not someone but some THING," Kelly Meadows answered. "Thank you for your input. We're running this story tonight on the ten o'clock news."

Mom laid on the couch and moaned for the better part of an hour. Dad juiced fruits and vegetables in the kitchen like a mad scientist in an attempt to revive her with a green glass of gloop. It didn't work.

"That star is irreplaceable. It was made by one of the founding fathers of this town. What will his descendants say? Why would the monster want the star? What does that monster have against Christmas anyway?" Mom wiped tears from her eyes.

Then both their cell phones rang and I went to bed while Mom and Dad spoke in hushed tones to friends and neighbors until midnight.

Chapter Twenty-Two

Tuesday morning, December 2, went like this... On the bus to school, I couldn't help but notice that Joel was wearing all black, like some sort of ninja. He was wearing a black turtleneck shirt with black athletic pants. I think he would have put black ash over his face if he thought he could get away with it. Needless to say, he was not blending in.

Several police cars sped by us as we drove past the court house. Yellow crime scene tape circled the manger scene. Police dogs worked the court house lawn.

School was crazier than ever as well. Coach McGrath convinced one of the dog handlers to bring in a blood hound to sniff out his whistle, but Mr. Jameson commandeered the dog for his own purposes. Gertie the guinea pig was missing. Piper immediately organized the Glitterati and within minutes, posters were all over the school announcing Gertie's plight plus a reward of $4.27. Coach McGrath was not pleased with the recent events regarding Gertie's whereabouts. First of all, the Glitteri took down all of his posters of his beloved lucky whistle to put up their own. Second of all, the focus of finding his whistle had now been replaced with a frenzied urgency to locate the guinea pig before Frogman or the Chupacabra found it.

It was disturbing to see just how upset the Glitterati were, as if I would eat Gertie. Even Piper looked very afraid.

"Do you think I'm a monster?" I whispered to Artie when he was at his locker between classes.

"Monster? Like what kind of monster?" Artie whispered back.

"Are you serious? I am talking about me turning into a full-fledged monster. Do you think the whole town, Piper, and my mom are right about being afraid of me?"

"Okay, I think that eating bugs is super gross, but people around the world eat bugs too, like in the Amazon jungle." Artie shivered as if someone put a spider down his shirt. "But no, eating bugs doesn't make you a monster, just repulsive."

"I'm repulsive? Thanks, man!" I fumed.

"No, not you, but what you eat." Artie covered his mouth as if her were about to throw up just thinking about chewing on a cricket. "Come on, we'll be late to class."

By third period, more girls were crying in the hallways as rumors spread of a break-in at school during the previous night. Rumor had it that Frogman, working in partnership with the Chupacabra, had broken inside the school and stolen Gertie. At first the bloodhound seemed to be on the trail of the scent. But it turned out the dog had followed the first few kids that realized Gertie was missing. They had handled the cedar chips looking for Gertie as if she could really hide in an inch of bedding. The bloodhound searched the school with his handler. The handler reported back to Mr. Jameson in front of his fourth period class to give the grave news.

"It does appear that someone is responsible for Gertie's disappearance. My dog can't get a lead on a scent because she was taken. If she had crawled across the floor, he could have tracked her. But if she is carried away then my dog is unable to do his job. She was absolutely abducted!"

The crazy factor continued to hit new heights by the end of fifth period, as policemen strolled the halls and looked into the ceiling tiles and air ducts. The Glitterati were thrilled to have so much help to return Gertie back home to her exercise wheel and celery. But it wasn't Gertie, they were looking for. Joel and I saw two detectives check the locks on doors that led to the outside as Principal Evans rubbed his chin, looking somber.

Out in the hallway, Artie looked grim. "Wow. Good thing you've been laying low. This is bad enough."

"Yeah, I don't think the police are looking for Coach McGrath's whistle." I watched as one police officer moved away from the locks to inspect the hinges of the doors."

Joel walked right past us. If the police are looking for suspicious characters, Joel should have been suspect number one. He followed CJ through the hall, staying at least three students behind, and dodged behind trash cans, doors, corners, and water fountains. He completely stood out, especially since he wore black sunglasses in every class.

On our bus ride home, Joel, Artie and I sat together. Joel spoke in the most muffled tones as he read from his top secret journal. He flipped open his tablet and read the accusing evidence against CJ that he had gathered that day.

"CJ comes to class completely unprepared. Who doesn't bring a pencil to school? If pencils belong anywhere on this planet, it's in a school. He clearly thinks he's above us! 98% of all junior high students agree that it's not beneath them to use a pencil, but clearly, he does... It's very suspicious behavior, for sure." Joel waved his own pencil in front of my face.

"Wait, there's an actual poll about pencils?" Artie's eyes widened with surprise.

"I am very confident that if some university did do a poll about pencils, the numbers would be very high. It's just common sense." Joel licked his finger as he turned page after page in his journal. He continued on.

"He borrowed a pencil from Piper and if that wasn't bad enough, put the eraser in his mouth five times. Then he dug into his ear with his left pointer finger for 27 seconds. I can only assume this was done to scratch the vermin that lives in his earhole. He then put those terrible ear germs all over that same pencil. Poor Piper had to ask for her pencil back at the end of class. He would have stolen it. That's criminal behavior. He is not chivalrous. He is no gentleman. And he failed at least five times today to push his chair in. Clearly, he has no manners. I think you'll agree that criminals have no manners. He doesn't care about hygiene," Joel took a deep breath and folded his hands together as if in prayer. "And now Piper is infected. I dare say, she is lost to us forever. Alex, I would find a new love."

Joel looked at me with such deep felt sorrow, I thought I was going to punch him. Artie put his hand on my shoulder to calm me down.

"One more thing, Kevin and Randy must believe CJ to be of fraudulent character as well. They are surveying his every move. I believe those two will back up my findings." Joel closed his journal.

"CJ is a jerk for sure. An even bigger jerk than Dirk, but coming to school without a pencil hardly makes you a corrupt community college drop out. He's still a sixth-grader." I tried to be a voice of reason.

Joel refused to accept my interpretation of his data.

Chapter Twenty-Three

I wasn't too happy about our basketball practice that afternoon. I got slammed to the floor twice and stepped on while CJ and Dirk targeted each other on the court. CJ and Dirk claimed they didn't see me. This, of course, was a direct result of Dirk and CJ's competition to prove who is the better ball player. Their struggle to be the best is becoming painful for the rest of us.

That night after Mr. Brandt walked me to the door (Artie stayed in the truck locking the doors at his father's instruction) I entered my house to find another neighborhood meeting in the middle of my living room. This time, however, the number of attendees had doubled. There were two special guests. The first was our town librarian, Lydia Fisher, who gave a ten minute report on the history of Chupacabras in books and film. The second guest, was Jackie, CJ's mom. She was there to give us all an update.

"Unfortunately, nothing has been found thus far. While we are investigating four Chupacabra sightings at this point, there have not been any Frogman sightings. However, several of the camera traps in our area have been tampered with. The cameras appear to have been moved so that the lens is facing downward at the ground. Could this be Frogman? We don't have enough information at this point. Finally, I would like to commend Ellen and all of you for taking it upon yourselves to keep your neighborhood safe. Well done. Hopefully, things will be righted soon. In the meantime, remember to report anything suspicious." Jackie finished by giving everyone two thumbs up.

Mom dismissed the group with a strained smile, "Stay focused, stay alert, and God help us all." Everyone left and I went to bed listening to my mom check the doors and windows throughout our home.

Wednesday at school I realized that Joel had been right about one thing. Randy and Kevin were definitely watching CJ's every move. Dirk on the other hand, was laying low and keeping an eye on his book bag. While sitting in the dark during a DVD presentation in second period, I noticed that Kevin's jacket pocket had a hole in it. In fact, little tufts of fabric laid on the floor underneath where he sat at his desk. As I looked at those bits of fluff for another second, out of the corner of my eye, I saw Gertie. She was in the back corner of the room where the electrical cord of the DVD player connected into the outlet. Before I could move, Gertie clamped down on the cord and I heard a short sizzle noise as the projector screen went completely black. We were now sitting in complete darkness except for the thin line of light that crept from under the class room door. The class erupted into hoots and applause. I could still see Gertie with my night vision. For a second Gertie was stunned by the electric shock. But the loud commotion roused her, and Gertie skittered along the base board until she found an opening in a loose vent. In two seconds she was gone inside the walls of the school. Our teacher got up from her chair to stumble over to the light switch. Everyone booed as the lights were turned back on. Except Kevin and Randy. They noticed the bits of Kevin's jacket on the floor. Kevin jammed his hand into his jacket pocket only to find his fingers coming out the hole that Gertie obviously had made. He checked his other pocket to be sure that a small, furry rodent had not magically switched sides. Kevin and Randy looked completely surprised to think that Gertie would not have loved living in Kevin's jacket pocket. They glanced around the floor then looked over at CJ to see if Gertie had somehow made it into his jacket pocket.

Randy furrowed his brow and glared at Kevin. There was no doubt that he was upset with Gertie's flight to freedom. Kevin shrugged his shoulders and mouthed to Randy, "How was I supposed to know she would gnaw through my coat. Do you know how much trouble I'm in?"

Randy responded back, "He's the one who's supposed to be in trouble." He pointed slyly at CJ.

Really, this is incredible. There is no stealth with these guys. No one knew what happened because the class was focused on Mrs. Brodie who was trying to get the DVD player to turn back on. It took her a few moments to realize the cable cord was damaged and unusable.

Obviously, Kevin and Randy had abducted Gertie. They planned to plant her on CJ to make CJ out to be a thief. Meanwhile, I could hear Gertie's little nails scrape the inside of the air duct.

Two periods later, I detected a chewing sound above me as I walked the halls alone. I had left class to go to the bathroom but I really left to find Gertie. I listened against walls and then in the far distance of the hallway I noticed white flakes floating down to the tiled floor. Looking up I could see the small formation of a hole being chewed through a ceiling tile. It was Gertie and apparently, she was hungry.

I looked up and down the hall and with no one else in sight I did what I could do without worrying about security cameras in the hall. I walked toward the suspicious tile and right before I was to walk under it, I flicked my tongue up at the ceiling tile knocking it lose from its frame. The tile was tilted and a small crack where the tile no longer held in the frame was just large enough for Gertie to fall through and land in my hands. It happened so fast I hoped no one watching this particular security camera would ever notice. I carried Gertie back to Mr. Jameson's class cuddling her in my arms. By the beginning of next period, it was all over school that Gertie had been found and that I had rescued her. Piper smiled at me, CJ rolled his eyes at me in the hallway, and Mr. Jameson thanked me profusely offering me celery sticks. Kevin and Randy frowned at me for the rest of the day.

Principal Evans took a different tack. He called me into his office. "Well, well, well, so here we are again. First it was Mrs. Mears stolen Spanish tests and now you have rescued Mr. Jameson's beloved lab rat." "Sir, no disrespect, but Gertie is a guinea pig."

Principal Evans nostrils flared and I could see he had recently trimmed his nose hair, but I didn't know which was worse; the well-groomed nose hair, the accusations, or that he made air quote signs with his hands every other second. For ten minutes, he accused me of kidnapping Gertie for attention, for fun, out of boredom, to upset students and staff, and to add to the chaos that had taken over our town of Cedarville. He also wanted to know if I knew about Frogman and his diabolical plans for Coach McGrath's whistle.

I sat silently across from him trying not to laugh, smirk, side-eye, sneeze, cough, yawn, inhale, exhale, or twitch. I avoided anything that would be misconstrued as discourteous toward Principal Evans and his crazy rantings. He crinkled his forehead and stared with unblinking and annoyed eyes. Was he trying to bore holes into my own eyeballs while gaining a confession from me that I had stolen the tests and kidnapped Gertie? It didn't work of course. After 90 seconds Principal Evans blinked and rubbed his eyes. He took a small bottle of eye drops out of his top desk drawer and squeezed the liquid into both of his eyes.

"I'm letting you go this time. But know this, you're under surveillance." He wiped at the little rivers of saline that were running down his cheeks. "That's right. I'm keeping my eyes on you. You think being helpful isn't suspicious? Ha! I'm on to you. Now go back to class."

Out in the hallway, I saw Libby.

"Nice going. Maybe you're not the worst booger eater ever. Maybe in fifty years Piper will forget all about you eating Dirk's snot and will remember you fondly as finding our school's favorite rodent." She smacked her gum and walked to class.

How does she do that? She can take something so positive and make it absolutely horrible. That is her super power. Draining the goodness out of any circumstance. I, of course, could only hope that Piper would be able to forget that I ate Dirk's boogers. Maybe finding Gertie would make her realize that there's more to me than just being the reigning champ of Fear Factor Friday. Deep down I hoped there really wasn't something wrong with me because who in their right mind would eat another person's snot?

On the bus ride home, Joel had Artie and I sit strategically on one seat so that we could go over his intel on CJ. Joel whipped out his notebook with his list of clues supporting his theory that CJ was a deranged sixth-grade hoaxer.

Here was today's list:

1.   He re-used a piece of tissue four times before depositing it into a trash receptacle.

2.   I caught him scratching his butt three times today.

3.   Again, he failed to bring a pencil or pen to school. He borrowed from Piper once more and this time did not give it back for the entire day.

4.   He failed to push in his chair in all classes that we attend together.

5.   Worst of all, he went to the bathroom and did not wash his hands.

"Do you understand how serious this is guys?" Joel looked from me to Artie then back to me. "He did not wash his hands! I think it is safe to say that the trash can, the bathroom, his locker, his desks, the doors and hallway walls that he touched today must be ripped out of the school and burned on a pyre lit with a flaming arrow shot from a safe distance of 100 feet away. Then those ashes should be collected by a trained professional and safely deposited wherever bio-hazard wastes go to die. After that, we must do it again tomorrow. The burning of things that have come into contact with him that is, except of course people, like, poor, poor, dear, sweet, Piper. She had a good life. She had it all; Popularity, friends, laughter, and silky brown hair until her luck turned against her when she came into contact with "him." Who knew that a single pencil could be a Weapon of Mass Destruction?"

Again, Artie put his hand on my shoulder to keep me from smacking my second best friend in the world. "Uhmm, you know, these things you witnessed today, still do not mean he's a vile, rogue spy working as a double agent for an enemy state. Maybe he's just an irresponsible kid with a lot of hygiene issues." I said, trying to offer up another theory. Joel slammed his journal shut in my face and looked out the bus window without saying another word to me. He did, however, talk to Artie as if I wasn't there.

"It seems to me that a person who lacks manners, sanitation skills, and believes he's above following the rules is a dissident."

"A what?" Artie and I both said at the same time. Of course, Joel turned to Artie to answer.

"A dissident is a person who does not conform to our rules and way of life in middle school." Joel folded his arms across his chest. "Any person, I know of, who doesn't conform to the rules is an adult who's paying their own way in life. Say if a guy wants to eat cereal over the sink in a coffee mug rather than a bowl at the table, who's going to stop him? Me, you? If he paid for the cereal himself and pays his own rent then, he does as he pleases. I know this to be true. My mom tells my oldest brother, Jase, all the time to eat like a civilized person. He's twenty-one. He goes days without brushing his hair. His apartment looks like a recycling project except he still needs to sort paper from plastic. He and his roommates only wash their clothes on the fifteenth of a month if it has the letter "R" in it. He reuses his socks as furniture dusters when girls come over. Jase is an adult. Being an adult is gross, and hence, that is CJ; and CJ is no kid. I tell you, I know that of which I speak."

It was hard to argue that Jase did not indeed live outside the normal conventions of polite society. It was also hard to argue that CJ needed to learn a few manners, come prepared to class, and remember that soap is his friend. Yes, they were both gross, but I still had a hard time believing that somehow CJ had fooled everyone, especially his own mother, and registered at West Ridge Middle School as a sixth-grader. Joel is convinced CJ has a driver's license and shaves twice a day.

Once off the bus and assisted home by my mother, it was time to change into my basketball uniform to go to my first game. By the way, we were massacred. We were chewed up, stomped on, then thrown out with yesterday's garbage. Why did we lose 54 to 2? I will tell you...Dirk, Randy and Kevin continued their game of keep away from CJ. They weren't interested in scoring. For them winning meant never letting CJ have the ball, therefore Hank's Hardware hammered us into oblivion. Finally, Mr. Brandt was so angry he took those four out of the game and put Artie and I in for rest of the game. It was such a blood bath. For real! Artie fell 29 times. His elbows, left knee, and his bottom lip were bleeding. I fell eleven times—bleeding from my right ear, both knees and had a huge bruise on my lower back. The only points we scored were in the first 90 seconds of the game when Dirk went in for a lay-up. That was it. Super humiliating.

Once at home, I took over the bathroom. That's right. Nobody cared because I stunk so bad from all that running. I started the water and flopped into the tub. It was so good to just be my froggy self. I could have stayed there all night. But after an hour, Libby pounded on the door.

"There are other people in this house, you know. Get out!!!" I could hear her smacking her gum on the other side of the door. I got dressed for bed and went to the living room to tell my parents, "good night."

They were on the couch watching the news. It was already ten o'clock. There was Kelly Meadows beaming with excitement. From the court house lawn she gave an update about the missing star. An image flashed onto the television screen. It was a picture, captured at night, of the star next to a sign that read, "Galaxy Bowling." Our star apparently had left its position at the manger set and decided to visit our one and only bowling alley. The star allegedly wrote to Kelly Meadows claiming it needed a little fun and was just going to wander about like the star in the Bible. Then it left a hash tag #followthestar and that was it. I thought my mother's head was going to explode.

Another reporter stood outside the bowling alley interviewing league players, the owner, and several police officers. There were no witnesses to the star's outing to the alley and it was now long gone.

Chapter Twenty-Four

The next morning at school, Dirk's homework was missing again. It wasn't really a mystery or a surprise. CJ scooted his desk as close to Piper's desk as he could. Then he borrowed her pencil. We were told to work in groups and you guessed it, CJ made sure he was in Piper's group. I was in Dirk's group. Dirk was really upset because his grades were dropping and now he had missed more assignments. I told him to write out what he could as others in our group worked on the current project. I helped him rewrite his missing assignment.

"Why are you doing this?" Dirk asked suspiciously.

"Because I don't think you're losing your assignments." I corrected some spelling mistakes. Dirk it turns out is not a champion speller.

"Yeah, I don't know how he's doing it?" Dirk glared across the room at CJ who gave a slight smirky-smile and a head nod back at him, which only made Dirk grit his teeth.

"Ignore him. That's what he wants." I quietly suggested to Dirk, as I rewrote one of his sentences. He had misplaced a prepositional phrase.

"How? He's such a humongous jerk-face."

"Look, he's going to get caught. He's going to slip up. They always do. Remember when you cut off my shoe laces in fourth grade right before our Sports Day relay race? I couldn't run and Lance had to take my place. But later that day you got in trouble. Why? Because you forgot to throw away the laces and they were hanging out of your pocket!"

"Oh, yeah..."

"Then in third grade you kept farting and pointing at me in class so I got in trouble. You did that for four days until the teacher couldn't ignore the stinky smell anymore and she sent me to the nurse's office. My mother wouldn't let me eat anything with sugar in it for a month. But you tried again on the fifth day and what happened? You took off running to the bathroom and without a hall pass."

"Oh, man..." Dirk cringed.

"Again, in third grade, you put a wad of chewed bubble gum in my chair. I sat in it and what happened next?"

"Okay, okay, point made," Dirk winced again. He was quiet for a few seconds more, then barely above a whisper I heard, "Sorry."

I could have keeled over right then and there. What was happening? Were we bonding? Were we becoming friends? Had Earth's poles flipped and now south was north and north was south? Was it still Thursday? Had I entered another dimension where...
I got popped in the eye with a wadded piece of paper.

It really burned. I think it scratched my cornea.

"Hey, my homework assignment? Remember? You've been staring off into space for like, forever? What's wrong with you? Are you crazy?"

"Uhmmm, no." I could only see through one eye. My other eye was tearing up non-stop.

"Seriously, you're crying now?" Dirk smirked.

"You don't remember hitting me in the eye just now?" I tried to blink away a tear.

"Oh, wow... It's just sorta second nature, I guess. Sorry about your eyeball."

You would think that he would somehow show me some gratitude for saving his life. That's what makes this so hard for me, because I want to tell him he's alive because of me. Every time he hits me with a basketball or tries to murder my eye. I want to yell that he gets to enjoy being a jerk for another day because I rescued him. But he can't know about me. I can't tell him I'm the reason he's alive to enjoy sports and loath CJ's guts. I helped him finish his homework assignment and he thanked me by giving me a slight chin bob. It was very subtle but it happened. Dirk got five points off for turning it in late but it was only five points. It could have been worse.

Since the bloodhound was back on regular duty working the fields and neighborhoods of Cedarville, Coach McGrath had resorted to his Plan B. He borrowed his neighbor's dachshund named Heidi. This little dog had a pink collar decorated with rhinestones with one humongous pink flower attached to it. Coach McGrath held the pink leash, also decorated with rhinestones, and from afar it looked as if he was walking a giant blossom with a tail and four legs.

Coach McGrath undoubtedly felt his luck had suffered. Each finger on his hands were wrapped in band aids due to small cuts acquired by ruthless printer paper and other odd sorts of stationery. He became leery of paper. All kinds of paper; the newspaper, copy paper, paper towels, and toilet paper. Walking the halls with Heidi, he pulled her along the edges of the lockers where she stopped eight times and whined. With a master key to open any locker, he grew disheartened to find that Heidi alerted on dead, dried bugs crumpled in the far corners of the bottom row of lockers. He pulled out his new whistle and held it in front of her nose. She immediately ran up to the janitor's closet and whined.

He unlocked the door of the closet. Heidi barked and pulled at her leash. Coach McGrath began to smile as Heidi bounded over bottles of bleach, soap, and empty buckets. She lunged into a corner, knocking over mops, and dug with her nose sniffing the floor. Heidi stopped snuffling. Her tail wagged excitedly. "C'mon girl. Show me the whistle," Coach McGrath stepped over a vacuum cleaner to get a better look. In Heidi's tiny jaws she held a dead cricket. Then she didn't. Heidi swallowed the dried out bug.

"Are you kidding me? Are you kidding me?!" Coach McGrath bellowed in the hallway for all to hear. "This dog is defective! Why would anyone have a defective dog?!" Coach McGrath carried a whimpering Heidi out the front doors of the school and drove away.

I wished I had Heidi. She could sniff out a treasure trove of dead bugs for me. Bugs that I could eat and honestly, that's more important than a whistle if you ask me. I mean, I haven't had a good bug in forever. But Coach McGrath would disagree, because later that afternoon, I spotted him taping poster boards on several walls of the hallway. He had upped the finder's fee for his whistle to $125.00.

"You know, I could just go to the store and buy a new whistle for less than ten dollars and give it to him." Randy said to Dirk while we were within earshot of where they sat on the bus.

"It wouldn't work. Coach knows his whistle like the back of his hand," Artie whispered to me and Joel. "You couldn't trick him that easily. My dad says athletes can get real weird about superstitions."

"Speaking of weird," Joel cleared his throat and flipped open his journal.

"Here is today's list of condemning evidence against CJ:"

1.   Again, no pencil or pen. Since Piper was out of pencils, he borrowed from Julie.

2.   Wiped his nose on his sleeve twice.

3.   Coughed fifty-two times without covering his mouth.

4.   Cleared his throat twenty-seven times today. The sound was like a motorboat hung up on a flock of rubber ducks.

5.   Went to the bathroom after lunch and again, no washing of the hands.

6.   Socks look remarkably like the pair he wore yesterday. I doubt they have been changed.

7.   He gives crazy side-eye whenever Dirk is around. CJ watches Dirk like a buzzard watches a moldy ham sandwich in the middle of the desert.

8.   Randy and Kevin are still watching CJ. There is no doubt about it.

"As I said before, everything he comes into contact with, must be destroyed by fire, except humans and animals," Joel flailed his hands about. "This community is at a far greater risk than I first believed. We must band together and stop his one-man campaign of polluted pathogens."

I didn't know what to say. Randy and Kevin definitely looked for revenge, but as much as Joel watched CJ, he had yet to discover CJ taking Dirk's homework assignments. All I could think was this: it must be happening in a class where Dirk and CJ are present but Joel is not. Otherwise, Joel would have seen this and would not hesitate turning CJ into the teacher, Principal Evans, Police Chief Carlton, and the State's Attorney's office. CJ must be getting Dirk's homework immediately in the mornings before class.

That afternoon, basketball practice consisted of a two mile run around the gym. Then CJ and Dirk were paired up to play against me and Randy. Dirk kept changing up the teams so that he was playing against CJ. After a "pep" talk from Mr. Brandt, Dirk finally started passing the ball to CJ. Except now, Dirk threw the ball directly at CJ's feet. Each and every time.

Chapter Twenty-Five

That night on the news, Kelly Meadows reported once more on the missing star. Another letter had been mailed to the television station addressed to her from the "star" with a photo included. The photo showed the star leaning against the bottom of a sign for Atomic Car Wash. Like before, the picture was taken at night. The owner of the car wash was interviewed along with employees. But the picture had been taken after the car wash closed. There seemed to be no witnesses. In other news, Kelly Meadows reported that Frogman and the Chupacabra were still at large.

All that night, I dreamt about bugs; Big ones, little ones, creepy, crawly, chewy, crunchy, and crispy ones; on top of ice cream, corn flakes, and pancakes.

Friday morning at school I kept thinking about my dream and all those insects Heidi found. By third period I couldn't concentrate on our lesson anymore.

Dirk was missing his pencil too, which I assumed was the pencil CJ was now using. Dirk was miffed. He borrowed a pencil from the teacher. Our teacher was not too pleased with Dirk's new routine of missing papers—and now pencils. I asked for a hall pass for the bathroom and quickly walked to the janitor's closet. The door was happily unlocked for the moment. I stepped inside, shut the door, and turned on the light. I stepped over buckets and brooms and peered into the corners of the closet. I snagged two dead crickets, popped them in my mouth and was immediately busted by the janitor.

"What do you think you're doing?" Principal Evans was not happy to see me again so soon.

"I saw that the janitor door was open and thought I would look for Coach McGrath's whistle. You had asked me about it so I thought maybe no one had looked there. Besides Coach McGrath just raised the reward for it."

"Are you blaming our janitors for his lost whistle?" Principal Evans leaned forward in his chair.

"No, not at all. It might have ended up there by accident. That's all."

Principal Evans looked very suspicious. "Go sit outside, while I decide what to do with you."

Outside his office in a narrow corridor I sat on a bench staring into the corners of the front office. Nope, no dead bugs anywhere. It appears the filthiest place in our school is definitely the janitor's closet. Coach McGrath came in, upset and holding seven silver whistles in his hand.

"This isn't working. The students keep bringing me brand new whistles to get the reward money. No one is looking for it anymore. These little rascals only care about money." Coach McGrath shook the whistles in his hand. The ladies in the front office offered their condolences. "Alex, what are you doing in here?" Coach was surprised to see me.

"Actually, I was looking for…"

"He's on his way back to class. Thank you, Alex for all your help." Principal Evans said standing in his office doorway. "Now go."

You didn't have to tell me twice. I was out of there.

After school, I had another basketball game. We played against First City Bank of Cedarville and it was another bummer. We lost 67 – 28. Why? This game Dirk and his minions passed the ball to CJ, but just out of arm's reach. They tried their best to look like they were including CJ in the game, but with their smirks and smiles, it was easy to see that it was all for the benefit of our coaches. Every once in a while, they would misjudge their throw and CJ would be able to get it. This is how we got 28 points on the board. Artie played only four minutes. I played six. I actually held the ball three times, because Dirk passed it to me. I was so confused by his friendly gesture of including me in the game that I just stood there and held the ball until the other team grabbed it out of my hands. As the other team kept ripping basket after basket, Artie never stopped smiling. It's his birthday tomorrow. He clearly was not in the game. The coaches were not happy, but at least they weren't fuming. The rest of our team looked like they wanted to bounce basketballs off of Dirk, Randy and Kevin's faces. They were done with their shenanigans.

But beyond that—I was done with the whole "our town is under attack" shenanigans. No one was allowed to leave the gym until everyone was ready. We gathered up all our equipment and were escorted to the parking lot by one of the parents on the other team. He was a police officer in uniform and directed us to our cars with his super-sized flashlight.

"See you tomorrow." Artie said, still smiling. "It's gonna be great!"

"Absolutely!" I called out as I reached my dad's car. My dad stood at the front of the car as a look-out while the rest of my family got in and quickly buckled up. Dad then rushed to get in the car as if the earth's surface was on fire.

"Whew! That was close!" Mom looked back at me, Libby, and Sam.

"Mom, we lost 67 – 28." I replied.

"No, hon. Getting to the car. I'm glad we made it."

I was really tempted right then and there to spill my guts; just to tell my family about the weird frog on the beach, my funky feet, and how I was the elusive "Frogman." But I decided against it when Dad said, "I think whatever it was has really moved along. With all of this activity in town, it's long gone by now."

"I sure hope so. It's completely wrecking my eighth-grade year. This is so unfair that I can't go outside, to the mall, or hang out at Deja Brew Coffee House," Libby whimpered.

"I don't want you drinking coffee. Especially if it's not organic and fair trade." Mom turned around and glared at Libby. "You don't need it anyway. It will stunt your growth."

"Why does it matter anyway? With our town in lockdown, I no longer have the right, the choice to disobey. I no longer have the choice to make a good choice because all the bad choices have been ripped away from me."

At that, Mom and Dad were concerned. Dad jumped in. "Are you saying you want to do bad things and be disobedient?"

"No, not at all. I'm only saying that if I wanted to, I now can't. It's just so unfair." Libby sulked.

"Why don't I order vegetarian pizzas when we get home." Mom tried to lift Libby's spirit.

"Can we switch it up and order pepperoni and Canadian bacon pizzas with vegetables instead?"

"Sure." Dad chimed in. "That sounds great." I think he really misses real meat too.

"O.k. fine." Mom gave in.

After dinner, I worked on some homework until it was time for the news. Here was the lead story from Kelly Meadows. "I received another letter from the missing star again today. The star is enjoying its vacation and has been photographed in front of Solar Windows and Doors, right here in Cedarville. You will notice this picture has been taken at night as well. If you look closely, it appears to have a can of soda with it. We interviewed the owner of this company and her employees. No one witnessed the star posing for photographs at this establishment. In other news, no word still on Frogman or the Chupacabra but we are hearing from several sources now that some of the camera traps have been tampered with. The investigation is still underway. We will let you know as soon as we have any new information. Back to you, Tom."

What Jackie had reported to Mom's Monster Neighborhood Watch Group was true. Someone is tampering with the cameras, but why? The whole town is in hysterics. At that moment I didn't care. Tomorrow was Artie's birthday party. I would get to spend the rest of the weekend hanging out with my best friends.

Chapter Twenty-Six

Saturday morning, I awoke to the sugary scented goodness of cinnamon rolls in the oven. I jumped out of bed to find Mom and Dad rearranging furniture in the living room. Mom had called an emergency meeting of the Neighborhood Watch Group. Libby, Sam, and I were told that none of the good food was for us. It was for the guests when they arrived. Our living room filled rather quickly and Jackie was once again, the special guest. She reminded everyone, "Be aware of your surroundings and be extra cautious when going outside. It was reported to local police by hunters that more camera traps have been meddled with. Also, some of the food traps were dismantled. Unfortunately, we don't know what is going on yet." The room gasped with Jackie's revelations.

"Could it be raccoons, squirrels, or coyotes?" a neighbor asked.

"No, typically, raccoon, opossum, squirrel, and coyote don't eat a pizza and throw away the box. You need hands for that." Jackie stated.

"Then Frogman is still here. Frogman must have hands to have carried poor Dirk and Piper out of the Marshall house," another neighbor shuddered, clutching her purse.

Jackie relayed to the group that she didn't feel Frogman would know how to tamper with cameras. Though most of the group settled down, I could see my mom was more nervous than ever.

Artie's party started at 5 at Galaxy Bowling. Joel, Artie and I put on our bowling shoes when our entire basketball team walked in. That's right, Dirk, Kevin, Randy, and CJ and the rest of our team stood at the front counter getting their shoes and bowling balls. I couldn't believe it. Artie's dad ran up to the front counter and welcomed them all.

"What's going on? I didn't invite them." Artie looked nervous, upset, and confused with his right hand shaking rapidly.

"I think your dad is trying to call a truce between Dirk and CJ by inviting them to your birthday," I said.

"This is awful!" Artie grimaced.

"This is outrageous!" Joel seethed. I didn't know who was more upset because while Artie's hand quivered rapidly, Joel was the one huffing and puffing. He looked on the verge of hyperventilating.

"This is the worst birthday ever. Ever! Does my dad hate me? I guess I'm not good enough to be his son. He can't stand to spend time with me unless CJ and Dirk are around."

"No, that's not it. I think he's trying to build up the team." I offered.

"But it's my birthday. It's my party." Artie struggled to tie his shoe laces because his hands shook so badly.

Mr. Brandt beamed. He smiled so big, I thought he was auditioning for a toothpaste commercial. "Surprise! Look who's here!" Artie's dad swept his arms around as if he were unveiling a time machine. "Happy Birthday Son!"

In the weakest voice ever heard, Artie said, "Hey guys."

I smiled. I tried to anyways. Joel cupped his hands to his nose and mouth. He breathed slowly and deeply.

"Great! I'll set up the scoreboard. Let's get started!" Artie's dad clapped his hands together.

CJ and Dirk were definitely in competition to see who could make Artie's birthday really about them. It was a close call but CJ was in the lead. I had to say, this was a disastrous idea by Artie's dad. No one had rolled a ball down a lane, and they were already arguing over who had the best bowling ball in the entire galaxy, solar system, or universe.

But it didn't matter. Because who would have believed it: Artie killed it at Galaxy Bowling. Artie's mom, who showed up with the biggest cake ever, and his dad were in wide-eyed wonder and amazement as Artie rolled nothing short of 200 his first game. The crazy thing is, Artie hadn't bowled in years. The last time we went bowling was when our air conditioning went out at home one summer after second grade. Mom took us bowling so we wouldn't get bored, cranky, and pass out from heat stroke. But all I remember from that time was a lot of gutter balls.

After nearly two hours, Artie did it! He won every game. I had never seen him so on fire before. He is the Bowling Grand Master, the Ruler of the Twelve Alleys, King of all Lanes! He didn't just win, he blew everyone out of the water, including his dad. We were cheering. We were screaming, and high-fiving! His last game he scored 211. It was incredible. I got 147 on my last game, but who cares... Artie had the best day ever!

I only wish it lasted until midnight, or even until Sunday afternoon. I wish I had more self-control.

I wish I hadn't eaten one of his birthday presents. His mom bought him a new fish for their fish tank. Their tank is really kinda cool. It's a huge salt water tank. One that sits in the family room where Joel, Artie, and I played video games after we got back from bowling. This is where we were to sleep. All the other guys had gone home from the bowling alley.

The fish in question, was a blue tang. You know the one from those movies where that blue fish has memory problems? Artie had wanted one for a long time. I had trouble concentrating on the video games we had been playing. I found one dead spider in their house and happily disposed of it. But it made me so much hungrier for—you know, things one might find out doors and in a pond. I went crazy looking at those fish. When Artie and Joel went to the kitchen to get more cake, I couldn't resist. Artie took two steps into the family room and immediately knew something was wrong. He went straight over to the fish tank. He looked and looked for his new fish then slowly turned around to face me.

"Where's Spike?" Artie looked disgusted.

"Who?" I picked up the controller for the game we had been playing.

"You know, my new pet fish Mom gave me. The big blue one."

"Oh, I don't know. Let's take a look." I studied the tank from top to bottom.

"Oh, man, maybe another fish ate it. That's awful. Sorry." Joel patted Artie's shoulder offering his condolences.

"How? He was the biggest fish in the entire tank?" Artie glared at me.

"Maybe they all ganged up on him because he was the new fish. Maybe they all decided to have a big dinner. Sorry, man." Joel looked at all the smaller clownfish. "Who knew these guys were the ninjas of the sea."

"Yeah, who knew that I should have named him 'Sushi.' I think I'm going to be sick." Artie sat down on the couch and looked at his shoes.

I knew what I had done was inexcusable. I wish I could have barfed up Spike right then and there and all would be okay. I faked a head ache and went home. I felt awful but at the same time felt really hungry. After everyone went to sleep, I looked for bugs but there weren't any to be found in our house. I stayed awake long into the night to try to find a way to apologize to Artie. How could he ever forgive me? Maybe I really am a monster; one without fangs and claws but still an awful creature none the less. God please help me. The next morning at church, it was just me, the regular group of kids in our youth group, and CJ.

The next week Artie pretty much ignored me. Sure, we still sat together at lunch, but he didn't talk to me directly. Joel was still so busy spying on CJ that he never noticed that Artie and I had virtually stopped speaking nor that whatever was communicated between us was done through him. Coach McGrath's whistle was still missing and Dirk "lost" two more assignments. With the police onto the "heavenly" theme of the Star's local excursions, they were staking out "Owen Day Realtor," "Star Brite Car Wash," and "Night Owl Café." But the star had made other plans. Four times this week it mailed pictures of its vacation to Kelly Meadows where it was now lounging by one of our city pools, sitting in a rusty chair outside an antiques store, leaning next to the ticket booth at the drive-in theater, and propped against the bottom of a slide at one of our city parks. I thought my mom might lose her mind. Mom began her own search for the star, waking right before dawn and driving the streets of Cedarville.

While Libby, Sam and Mom went Christmas shopping at the mall this week after school, Dad and I dug the Christmas tree out of the attic and put it up. We also brought down her six crates of snowmen. Her collection of snowmen rival her collection of fake pumpkins, by the way. But even with these jolly white snow people decorating our house and cluttering every flat surface, it still didn't feel like Christmas was only a few weeks away.

Christmas is my favorite holiday, but I didn't feel like celebrating. People were still afraid to go outside. Local and state police continued to look for any sign of a monster. Several news crews stayed in the area. Men had formed a club in town and named themselves, "TMW" for Texas Monster Watch. They drove around in trucks and searched private property for Frogman and the Chupacabra using burritos as bait.

Our basketball team played two more games and we lost. The grudge match between CJ and Dirk continued on as our coaches remained at a loss as to how to fix this problem. Artie bowled twice more this week. He invited Joel, but not me. I had to do something.

After a little talk with God, I knew what to do to make things right with Artie. I asked Mom and Dad for opportunities around the house to make some money. Mom was thrilled, Dad was pleased. I was disgusted. I cleaned all toilets in the house, and showers too, even the gunk between the bathroom tiles. I helped Sam clean up his toys. We went through them to see which ones we could donate to charity. I vacuumed, swept, mopped, wiped, dusted, and even washed Sam's blanket that he accidentally peed on. How do you accidentally pee on your favorite blanket? While I cleaned, Sam decided it was time to have a little talk with me.

"Will Frogman ever come back?" Sam pouted.

"I haven't gone anywhere. I'm still here, separating your collection of cars and trucks."

"Why won't you jump at your basketball game. You could win." Sam winged a car at me. I jumped to get out of the way.

"No throwing. And I can't just jump across the basketball court. No one will understand. It may upset some of them too, including Mom and Dad. Don't worry, once things settle down, we will be able to go outside again."

"And then you'll jump?"

"Yes, but only when no one is looking." Satisfied, Sam crawled onto his bed and took a nap.

That next Saturday, Dad took me to the pet store. With the money I made from all the chores plus the money I still had left over from finding that missing hairless dog in October, I bought Artie a new fish. I also bought thirty crickets to feed the new fish. Dad thought it was excessive but I sat in the back of the car and happily ate 28 of them on our way over to Artie's house. Dad waited in the car as I rang Artie's doorbell.

Artie opened the door. I handed him the plastic bag with the blue tang swimming around inside. Artie looked at it and then back at me.

"I'm very, very sorry for eating your birthday gift. I vow, here and now, to never, ever eat another one of your birthday gifts and/or pets."

Artie still looked suspicious. "How many fish were originally in this bag? It's almost dinner time. I'm sure you're getting hungry."

"There was only one. That's all I could afford." I handed him the brown paper bag with the last two surviving crickets inside. "However, there were originally 30 crickets in this bag but now there are two. See, no more fish. Just bugs for me." Then I accidently burped. I wasn't even trying.

Artie scrunched his face in disgust. "I will take your apology under consideration. We are decorating our Christmas tree right now so I need to go." I walked back to the car and felt hopeful that Artie would eventually forgive me. While I waited for Artie to accept my apology, teachers and students counted down the days until Christmas break began.

Chapter Twenty-Seven

Artie was still somewhat quiet around me but by Monday, December 15th, things were mostly back to normal. Except of course, Joel. There was nothing normal about Joel's anti-CJ agenda.

Here is part of Monday's list:

1.   Once again CJ comes to school unprepared for classes. He dared to copy Mandy's homework before class today. Again, criminal behavior.

2.   The tip of his nose is red. Probably from picking it!

3.   He slept for seven minutes in Math today. Who does that???

4.   He snorted snot nineteen times today and swallowed. I, on the other hand, gagged nineteen times every time he did it. So gross!

5.   He put his mouth all over the water faucet nozzle today in the gym. The whole school building needs to be hosed down with penicillin, borax, and a vinegar solution. He has contaminated the entire middle school athletic department.   Most of our coaches are over thirty with old, weak immune systems. I dare say, most of them, will probably die.

By Wednesday Joel's list of evidence expanded:

1.   CJ REFUSES to cover his mouth when he coughs, which shows his complete disregard for all human life!

2.   CJ's eyes are red and watery.

3.   His nose is now completely red.

4.   He reused the same piece of tissue five times today and stuffed it into his pockets.

5.   His cheeks are flushed.

6.   Most likely he is running a fever.

7.   He borrowed a pen from poor Lance Kramden today. I believe CJ is targeting his victims now. He is taking out the weakest first. I believe he has now

launched Phase 2 of his hideous plan to take over West Ridge Middle School.

8.   His germs are most likely mutating into a new form of biohazard this planet has never seen.

9.   Since I am the one who discovered this new disease and have recorded all the hideous symptoms, I am calling this infection "The CJ Syndrome."

10.   We may only have weeks to live.

Because Joel was so fixated on CJ he failed to notice that other students were coming down with the flu. It was running rampant through school, and our community at large. The next morning CJ came to school looking horrific. I knew today could be my only real chance at discovering what was happening to Dirk's homework and trying to find Coach McGrath's whistle. It was now a week before Christmas break. I didn't have much time to figure this out. Luckily, CJ looked half alive when he came into class early this morning. I hoped this would be easy. Here was my chance to do a little investigating without Joel watching CJ or me.

"Hey Man, you don't look too good," I offered as CJ slumped into his seat.

"Yeah, no…. I mean, yeah, not feeling too hot." CJ answered then coughed into the open expanse of the classroom. All I could think was that Joel was onto something here with CJ.

"You got something right here." I pointed to his nose. He really didn't, but this was my big plan to separate him from his backpack. A fake booger. Surely, he would go to the bathroom to wipe his nose and I could take a look into his pack for any hijacked homework that he might have taken from Dirk.

CJ looked up at me. "Oh, man." Then wiped his nose across his sleeve. Okay, so my big plan to find Dirk's homework didn't work. Not even close. Joel was definitely right about this one. CJ has issues, hygiene issues. I had to try again.

"Nope, not even close. Oh, look. Here comes Piper." I pretended to see her behind him. CJ covered his nose and mouth with both hands and ran to the bathroom. As fate would have it, Joel followed him out of the room. I grabbed my folder and casually knocked his backpack off his chair with my arm.

"Oh, no..." I muttered trying to act like this was really an accident. Then I bumbled around for a few seconds scattering my papers out of my folder across the floor. As I pretended to clean up my mess, I quickly unzipped his pack. There was Dirk's homework right on top. I grabbed it and put it under my folder and set his book bag back onto his chair. How in the world did he already nab Dirk's homework when he looks like the walking dead?

I quickly slipped back into my seat. When it was time to turn in our homework, Dirk scrambled through his book bag looking for his paper. It wasn't there. I could see Dirk seethe with anger. The teacher began to give Dirk a disapproving lecture when I raised my hand.

"Excuse me. I found this on the floor. I think it belongs to Dirk."

Dirk gave me a sudden and shocked look. I handed the paper over to Dirk but as I did I turned my head to see CJ's reaction. He scowled at me, snatched his book bag and searched through it. Not finding what he wanted, he eyed me suspiciously while his nostrils flared. He reached into his bag again and pulled out a cough drop as if that was what he had been searching for all along.

After class in the hallway, Dirk wanted to know where I had found his homework. Not wanting to start another world war, and wanting things to cool down between CJ and Dirk so we might win a basketball game, I told him, "It was on the floor in the classroom. I found it when I dropped my folder. But I do have an idea, a plan to make whoever is messing with you to stop."

Suddenly, Kevin pushed me against the wall and Randy stood next to him. Kevin had a runny nose and snorted in my face.

"If you're messing with Dirk. I will make you eat my snot, Randy's snot and whatever I find on the bottom of my shoes. Got it?!"

Kevin really has anger issues. Didn't I just save Dirk's homework? Haven't I been helping Dirk with his homework when it was missing? It was like trying to make friends with a gorilla who has a burr on his butt. "Uhmmm. Look, do you want to hear my plan or not?" I turned to look at Dirk while ignoring the fact that Kevin's drippy nose was inches from my face.

"Leave him alone. He's been helping me." Dirk admitted. Randy and Kevin stepped back in surprise and that's when I saw CJ stare me down from the other end of the hallway.

"Thank you. So, look, your homework is taken almost as soon as you step through the school doors each morning. Do you have a computer with a printer at home?"

"Yeah, of course," said Dirk.

"My plan is that you print a second copy of your work. Put those copies in separate folders in your book bag. One in the front and one in the back. Whoever it is will give up, because you're onto him."

It wasn't a glamourous plan. It wasn't full of spy technology. Surely Joel would have come up with something more daring, but I believed it would work.

Besides CJ has to know I am onto him now. I seriously doubt he believed me when I said I found it on the floor. Hopefully, he understands I can rat him out whenever I want to. But there were two reasons why I had to keep this to myself.

1.   Artie and I are just beginning to be best friends again. When I told him that CJ (who we suspected) was the one messing with Dirk and his homework, Artie asked me not to bust him because of his dad. Not CJ's dad, but Artie's. It turns out that Artie's dad is super frustrated with how the boys behave on the team. He says that this might be his first and last time to coach middle schoolers. Even though I thought this would make Artie happy to no end, he decided that having his father coach him is not the worst thing in the world. If Dirk knows CJ is definitely the culprit, Artie fears that Dirk, Kevin and Randy's behavior will cause his father to quit, thus canceling the basketball workshop during Christmas break.

2.   The second reason is really quite absurd. If I turn CJ in for stealing Dirk's homework which caused his grades to fall, I will literally be in trouble. I mean real trouble. More trouble than CJ would ever see. Principal Evans will not tolerate me being helpful one more time. He's totally suspicious of me and if he even thinks I am being considerate, accommodating, and kind, that's it for me. I'm sure I will wish I was back on Joel's radar. Besides, if Joel finds out, he will alert Principal Evans, the School Board, and the State Police. It won't be good.

Chapter Twenty-Eight

Friday morning, Dirk took my advice. When the teacher asked for his homework, sure enough, his report was missing. Luckily, he had printed another copy of his paper and was able to turn the second copy of his work in to the teacher. I couldn't help but notice that CJ never looked over at Dirk. Not one glance, not one twinge of a look.

Then I overheard Randy tell Kevin that today was the day Christmas was coming early for CJ. Kevin patted his right hand pocket of his jacket and Randy grinned fiendishly. Kevin reached into the same pocket and pulled out the slightest bit of blue cording. It had to be Coach McGrath's beloved whistle.

Instead of lying about finding it and getting a reward for it, they would rather frame CJ. I should have known that Kevin and Randy were involved.

But this was a problem for me and Artie. If I could help calm things down between all of them so that our basketball team wasn't divided into factions, maybe we could win a game and Artie's dad wouldn't give up coaching our team. Plus, I am really tired of losing each and every game. We should be first in the league. We have several of the best players. I knew what needed to be done. I would steal the whistle from Kevin and return it to Coach without him knowing who had it or who returned it.

At the beginning of gym class, we lined up in our rows while attendance was taken. Everyone stood in their lines except Randy and Kevin. I had a feeling they used this time to set up CJ. They returned to class and looked straight ahead, not one glance at each other, or toward Dirk. They stepped into their row and continued their forward stare as Coach McGrath counted their presence. He then tossed his clipboard aside and clapped his hands together. They tried not to be noticed but their oddball silence made me super suspicious.

"Ok, gentlemen. Today we go to war. Today we fight! Today we will divide into two teams for Dodge Ball! Owen, Artie and Cole, go grab the balls and rope to divide the gym." It was at this time, while Artie and the other guys trotted off to the storage closet that I approached Coach McGrath and faked the world's worst case of diarrhea. I quickly explained how my mother made me drink green juice for breakfast and now it wants revenge."

"Yeah, kale is something else! Just be thankful you're not throwing it up and experiencing the healing powers of kale twice. Get going and best of luck." Coach slapped me on the back and I ran back to the locker room. I spent the first few minutes looking up, down, and underneath rows of lockers, benches, and toilet stalls. The sinks and showers were empty as well. Not one whistle. I peeked through the window of Coach's office and saw CJ's backpack laying on his desk with the whistle cord wrapped around a shoulder strap. This was Randy and Kevin's big plan. Now I needed to do what had to be done. I grabbed the book bag and stole the whistle.

This way CJ would not be framed for stealing, and Kevin and Randy's plot to get CJ back for swiping Dirk's homework would fail. And above all, Artie's dad would not quit coaching us. I knew I needed a miracle if Dirk and CJ were ever going to get along on our team.

I grabbed up CJ's backpack, turned around and there was Coach McGrath watching me. "What are you doing in my office? I thought you had diarrhea? I came in to check on you because, well, you ate kale."

I tried to hide the whistle. I threw CJ's back pack over my shoulder like it was my own. I was stuck. Coach McGrath crossed his arms and waited for an explanation. I hopped from one leg to the other and locked my knees together as if my insides were about to explode. He wasn't buying my routine.

"Why are you in my office?"

"Uh, uh, well," I panicked and not just a little bit either. I lost all sense of reason and handed him his whistle. He nearly took my fingers off my hand as he snatched the whistle from me. Who knew he could be so grabby? I recoiled my hand and rubbed my fingers together. I had no idea what I was going to say.

"My whistle! My precious, awesome, good-luck whistle! Where on earth did you find it?!!" Coach McGrath held it up and looked at it in the light examining his whistle from every angle.

I was now, exactly where I didn't want to be. Sure, Coach McGrath was the happiest man alive. Sure, I just heard him use the word 'precious.' Sure, he paraded me out in front of the entire gym class and announced to everyone how I had found his whistle. Yes, he handed me a crisp, one hundred dollar bill, along with five crisp ten dollar bills, while everyone gaped at me. Especially CJ. I still had his backpack strapped across my shoulder. I should also mention at this point Kevin and Randy looked furious and a bit confused. I tried to shake off my fear by telling myself that they probably had kale for breakfast too.

"It was all a blur really." I stammered and began to sweat. Principal Evans eyeballs were protruding, PROTRUDING, out of his eyeball sockets. I grew a bit sick to my stomach. I worried one of his eyes might fall out, bounce across the desk, and glare at me until

244

I confessed everything, including my big "Frogman" secret.

"I'm sorry, I'm a bit confused. Why are you questioning my son as if he's done something wrong?" My mom held her purse in her lap and tapped her fingers across it as if she were beating on a tribal war drum. "You see, I was called away from an important meeting with the Historical Society. The star on the court house lawn was stolen. And as we addressed that critical situation, I dropped everything to come down here, to meet with you and my son, only to find out that he did something nice today for someone. But somehow that goes against a direct order you gave him?"

"Alex, please repeat for your mother where you found the missing whistle?" Principal Evans realized he probably shouldn't have called my mother.

"I told Coach McGrath that I found his whistle under a locker in the locker room." I wasn't lying about this. I did tell Coach that is where I found his whistle.

"Uh-huh. How do you think the whistle got there?" Principal Evans lips curled inward. It was not a good look on him.

"I don't know. Maybe it fell to the ground and kids accidently kicked it under the lockers. I'm not really sure." I tried to look as innocent as I could.

"So, what you're saying is... for all this time, after Coach McGrath along with the janitors and a police dog searched this school, you found it just lying in the open. And the whistle was near his office. And you found it on the DAY he happened to change his reward to $150.00. Really?"

"Well, I wouldn't say it was exactly out in the open."

"And you noticed this because you had diarrhea?" Principal Evans asked with the underlying conviction that he was dealing with a future convict. Unfortunately for Principal Evans, he just mentioned one of my mom's FAVORITE words.

"What?! Are you okay? What color was your DIARRHEA? Like how much? Would it fill a cereal bowl, or say, my purse? Are you running a fever?" Mom's hands went all over my face as she tried to determine if my fake diarrhea was fatal. "Principal Evans, why isn't he in the nurse's office? Don't you know the flu is going around!" She was really wound up now. "Oh, my poor baby..." Then she turned back to Principal Evans and let him have it. "I think one would be PLEASED to have a student as helpful as my son. Shouldn't that be our aim, to have students who look out for one another? I don't know why you think it suspicious that HE has been HELPFUL these past few MONTHS!!!"

Principal Evans couldn't speak, he just stared, moving his lips without any sound coming out.

"What? I can't hear you. DID YOU SAY SOMETHING?" My mom had lost all patience with Principal Evans and this meeting. She stood up and gently nudged me off my chair. She was convinced that I had the flu.

"No... I think we're done here. Let this be a lesson for us to learn," Principal Evans mumbled.

I had no idea what he was talking about. I think he was still hung up on his belief that all kids are guilty until proven innocent. My mom ignored what he said but finished with, "You'll understand that I am taking my son home now to recuperate from the FLU. GOOD DAY!"

Mom held me by the arm as we walked to the parking lot. Her eyes still darted to and fro as if we might be targeted by an incoming missile. She worried we could be attacked by Frogman or the Chupacabra in the middle of the day in front of my school. She talked about picking up Sam from the babysitter's when I looked to my left and saw Piper and her older sister, Paris, get into a car with their mother. I guess they have the flu too.

Chapter Twenty-Nine

By that evening, I knew Piper and her sister were not suffering from the flu or any other ailment. They were dismissed from school early because their lives were about to blow up all over the news. It turns out that the one who had been messing with certain camera and food traps was actually their mom. Yep! Piper's mom was at the precinct being questioned over her part in keeping Frogman free.

I knew all of this because once again, we had another emergency meeting of my mom's Monster Awareness Club in my living room. Every member stayed until midnight. Jackie was also present discussing the situation. It turns out that Mrs. Patterson, Piper's mom, thinks Frogman is actually good, and might even be a hero.

Mrs. Patterson was questioned by Kelly Meadows on the ten o'clock news. "I am not confessing to any crimes here. All I am saying is that I think we have it wrong with Frogman. He saved my daughter. I don't think he was trying to attack her or eat her."

Ewwwww! I had no idea people thought I was going to eat Piper. That was a new one. Of course, I would never attack her.

Mrs. Patterson continued, "I think my daughter was scared at first. But the fact is, she's alive because of him. I don't think we should hunt Frogman. Give him a chance." She then held up a small handmade sign that read, "#FreeFrogman."

Kelly Meadows looked so happy to have a twist in the case, she practically jumped up and down with excitement as Mrs. Patterson was taken away by Police Chief Carlton. But as Mrs. Patterson entered the Police Station, someone walked in front of her; A girl, carrying a blue book bag. It was Piper. Was she going to jail too? I didn't have much time to ponder if Piper would finish sixth grade in prison because the camera swung sharply to the left. There standing in front of a podium, dressed in a winter jacket, and wearing fake glasses was Joel.

He tapped the microphone to make sure it was on and coughed lightly into his hand, and began with, "Thank you for this opportunity to speak with all of you here this evening. I stand here tonight in sup-port of Mrs. Patterson, and her daughter. Speaking as the world's foremost authority on Frogman, I am in agreement that Frogman is not a threat to our community and way of life," Joel adjusted his fake glasses. "The facts are that Frogman saved two classmates of mine on that fateful Halloween night and I have pictures to prove it. It should also be noted that frogs only eat what they can fit in their mouth. There is no way that Piper or Dirk were in any real danger. The only danger for them was to remain in the attic of the burning structure. With temperatures as they are in December, Frogman has likely gone south to warmer climates or is in hibernation, which is why we do not have any more footprints or pictures of this creature. I am asking that all food traps be removed at this point as they are only giving wild animals diarrhea. Our town is coated in it. It's disgusting. It's almost Christmas. Christmas should not have a rancid smell to it. Follow me on Tweeter at #FreeFrogman. Go to my website and there you can show your support and buy one of these." Joel held up a baseball cap and a t-shirt with the name "Frogman" on it. "Be sure to follow me on social Media!"

I stayed up and watched the 11 o'clock news in the kitchen but I didn't see or hear any new information about Piper or her mother. In the living room, Jackie tried to assure Mom, Dad, and all of our neighbors that the police were not giving up on capturing Frogman and that Mrs. Patterson was most likely traumatized. She was sure of it since Mrs. Patterson wasn't making any sense. Then she mentioned that a strange new animal had been seen.

Immediately Mom looked like she was about to pass out. She turned pale with anticipation of this new information. Jackie told the group that we should be on the look-out for this strange creature reported only two days before. This new monster in town was described as a Chuparaccoon. The women gasped. My mom screamed.

The next morning, I woke up to find that #FreeFrogman was trending worldwide. Joel had 200,000 new followers on the internet and had sold out of t-shirts, coffee mugs, baseball caps, and pencils. Yeah, that's right, he now sells pencils, and autographed copies of his super blurry photo. I tried calling him, but his mom said he was meeting with Mrs. Patterson, Piper, and the Mayor of Cedarville.

Hanging up the phone, I got ready for our final game of league basketball. I knew it would be another depressing game. We had set a record for losses and the least amount of points accrued overall in our losing season. I showed up ready to sit on the bench but actually got to play for ten minutes along with Artie. Dirk no longer played keep away with CJ. Instead the new goal within the basketball game was throwing the ball at my back and feet. Apparently, Kevin and Randy tallied points in their new game each time they bounced the basketball off my body. Artie stayed near me and retrieved the ball several times. He actually made three baskets! This was huge! In the end, we still lost, but this time it was only by four points.

After the game, CJ wanted to know why I had his backpack during gym. He eyed me steadily with suspicion. I told him that in the excitement of Coach McGrath being reunited with his beloved whistle, I picked up the wrong back pack. I don't think he believed me. I just shrugged my shoulders and walked over to my dad as calmly as I could especially since Kevin and Randy had been watching me talk to CJ. They sneered at me as I walked past them and out into the parking lot with my dad.

I spent the rest of that Saturday monitoring Joel's website and Facelook page. He had uploaded three new 90 second videos walking around his neighborhood showing big blotches of poop on sidewalks, driveways, and in the road.

Joel was so busy that weekend that I never got a chance to speak with him or see him. He only sent me an instant message that read, "Super busy with meetings and phone calls. Piper and I are at dinner. Talk soon." Was this a date? Has the world turned upside down? Has the Earth's axis shifted? Artie had no idea if Piper and Joel had become the new "it" couple. He didn't care either. Nor was he concerned about Piper spending the rest of middle school in jail. He and his dad celebrated his six points from today's game by eating steak and fries with root beer floats at a diner. Afterward, I joined them at the bowling alley to watch Artie crush me and his dad with his mad bowling skills. He had the highest score of the night. While we were in the car, Artie's dad asked if he would be interested in forming a league for kids our age. I had never seen Artie so happy.

Chapter Thirty

With only two days of school left before our Christmas break, Joel remained undeterred in proving that the only thing in Cedarville that we should be careful, cautious, and mistrustful of was CJ.

On Monday and Tuesday we were missing many students due to colds, the flu, or early vacations. Yet, CJ was still at school coughing and wiping his nose on his jacket's sleeve.

Joel's list from both days looked like this:

1.   CJ is a biohazard. Why isn't the Center for Disease Control interested in this germ-infested specimen?

2.   What is the number for the Center for Disease Control? The school nurse most likely has the number on a poster hanging in her office.

3.   I called the CDC in Atlanta. They are already closed for the Christmas holiday.

4.   I told my theory to the school nurse about CJ being patient zero, that he was carrying a new disease the likes the universe has never seen.

5.   I also shared my other theory about CJ with the school nurse. I asked to see his file with his dental records as that would prove he is a community college drop-out.

6.   School nurse asked if I was on any medications and sent me back to class.

7.   CJ slept through a movie shown in English class. He drooled all over his desk.

8.   Everyone is excited about Christmas and the days off from school except CJ. He actually looks surly. How can anyone hate Christmas? How can anyone not be happy about having time off from school?

9.   CJ just found out that I had dinner with Piper. He looks mad. This is awesome!

10.   He has given me several suspicious looks. I wonder if he knows I am writing about him?

Piper was not at school those two days. Her mother was still on the front page of the paper and reporters camped out in front of their house. Dirk was at school and dodged questions from curious classmates. During lunch, Randy and Kevin seized control of the situation. They created an impromptu press conference in front of the podium that teachers use to make announcements in the cafeteria. Kevin grabbed the microphone, turned it on and blew into it. Everyone jumped. Dirk went up to the podium. He took the microphone and instantly had everyone's attention, including mine. "There's a lot of talk out there about what happened to me and Piper. Everyone's been asking me the last several days to comment. This is all I am going to say...Frogman is not like you or me. It had horrible eyes, fangs, and claws. If it is still out there, it needs to be captured. Anything that horrible, can't be good."

Joel was immediately seething. "So, by Dirk's estimation, bats are bad. Well, they keep the mosquito population in check. I can't wait to tell Piper about this!"

"Yeah, so what is going on with you and Piper?" I tried to ask as casually as I could.

"All I will say is that her family and I are working together to educate the world about Frogman. Do evil beings risk their life to save others? Think about it. And I really doubt it had claws. I would have seen them in the footprints I cast," said Joel.

That night, Dirk's quote was used on the local news and spread worldwide. Someone used their phone in school to record his statement. Then Joel was interviewed right after Dirk's clip by Kelly Meadows. Joel completely blew Dirk's statement right out of the water. He brought up how bats eat mosquitos and asked Kelly which animal in North America was the deadliest. Kelly quickly said the Grizzly bear. Joel refuted her guess with the truth, though it is an animal with eyes, claws and fangs. It's the cat, the feral cat to be exact. Cats kill more mammals, birds, and reptiles than any other animal in our country. No other animal comes close. "Are cats really monsters?" Joel looked over the top of his fake glasses he was now wearing to all interviews. "I don't think so. Besides the foot prints I found of Frogman did not have claws. Frogman is not a threat. Merry Christmas Everyone!"

Chapter Thirty-One

The unfortunate thing was my mom was not convinced by Joel. Joel, as a matter of fact, helped me to realize that I was not, indeed, a monster. Mom just thought Piper and her mother were both too distressed to see the truth and that Joel, was well...a sixth-grader without any advanced degrees to his name.

Christmas morning we had breakfast while Dad read the Christmas story to us from the Good Book as he calls it. When it was time to open gifts, it wasn't surprising to find that after two sweaters, socks, jeans, and a jacket, that I got a drone. And not just any drone. It had a camera! Within seconds, Mom had it out of the box and examined the camera. She gushed about how much fun I would have flying this thing over our house and neighborhood. It was then I realized how truly scared my mom had become. The drone was really for her. I was to perform several fly-overs that day to make sure no Frogman, Chupacabra, or even the newly named Chuparaccoon were enjoying their Christmas day by rambling around our subdivision. After three flights of the drone, Mom settled down and continued our Christmas tradition of tofu ham with every single green vegetable known to mankind. I, of course, would have gladly eaten the fake ham if only it had been served with a side of wriggling maggots and gravy. But I ate that phony ham just so I could get to the pies. That's when disaster struck!

Our door bell rang. Mom came in from the kitchen toward the front door, all smiles, and in a singsong voice said, "Everyone be on your best behavior. Jackie and her kids are here to join us for dessert."

Why, oh WHY does my mom always have to be soooooooo NICE!!! I was furious! This had now become the worst Christmas ever!! And it's not because I got clothes for presents and Mom bought herself a drone but wrapped it up for me. And it's not because Sam wouldn't let me sleep in and was jumping on my bed at six a.m. ready to unwrap presents, which by the way, he got all toys and a pair of pajamas. Libby got jewelry, and a whole bunch of clothes. But she loves clothes. She was so happy with her sweaters you would have thought that my parents had stuffed her stocking with pirate treasure! But it wasn't the worse because of any of this. It was the worst because THEY were HERE!

CJ sat at our dining table. If he so much as sniffles towards our pies, I told myself, I will barf up that fake ham all over him. Mom, however, learned her lesson. She cut the pie into slices away from CJ. I really didn't want to talk to him. I could tell he really didn't want to talk to me either. Katie was even quiet. She looked at Libby's new earrings, as Libby flipped her hair side to side. I think she was trying to flirt with Ryker. Ryker did his best to ignore Libby and stared ahead at Katie.

Mom and Jackie came to the table and distributed the pieces of pie before us but quickly disappeared back into the kitchen. They came back out with mugs of hot chocolate each with a candy cane poking up above real marshmallows. I knew something was up immediately. It's not uncommon for my mom to indulge us on Christmas but she never serves up chocolate pie and then offers a chocolate drink to go with it. Libby also was instantly suspicious. She quit flipping her hair and looked at each person at the table inquisitively, as if trying to read a code, a hidden cypher across our faces. Not able to crack the code, Libby concentrated her code-cracking efforts on Mom. She was right. Mom was the weak link here. She can't keep secrets for long. Something was up. Libby looked at me with a puzzling glance and we both gave Mom our full attention.

At this point, there were several things that could be said decisively about this situation. I got the smallest piece of chocolate pie and CJ got the largest. Ryker is horrible at making small talk. He actually asked my mom if the police had found the stolen star and if they thought Frogman took it.

Mom turned pale white. "Uhmm, thank you for asking. No, no word yet on where the star could be. The Historical Society and I had hoped it would have been returned last night or this morning. That would be the right thing to do. After all, it is the Christmas Star."

"I'm sure it will be back soon. It probably was bored and went... to the beach or something. I wish we could go to the beach." Ryker said digging into his slice of pie.

My mom cocked her head side-ways at Ryker, smiled slightly and returned to the kitchen. But something else was still wrong. It wasn't until Jackie returned to the kitchen to clean up with Mom that I overhead why everyone was so glum. I immediately went to call Joel but he wasn't home. He was over at Artie's. After I was able to get Artie and Joel on the phone, I learned that Joel had already discovered one of CJ's biggest secrets. When he knew he couldn't get CJ's file in the nurse's office, he realized someone else would have information on CJ. And that someone was Mr. Brandt. Joel decided to drop by Artie's to grab an application for the new bowling league that Mr. Brandt was forming.

While Mr. Brandt napped in his favorite chair, Joel and Artie snuck into Mr. Brandt's home office. On his desk was Mr. Brandt's file on Artie's basketball team. Joel scooped it up and Artie snatched it from him, but together they read that CJ's birthday is the day after Christmas and that he is a year older than them. CJ really should be in seventh grade. Joel felt completely vindicated in his suspicions of CJ, even though he wasn't a college graduate, CIA operative, or internet video star doing research for a new App.

What Joel and Artie didn't know, but I had just found out after accidentally walking into the kitchen at the wrong time, was that CJ's dad wasn't coming home. CJ's parents were getting divorced. Jackie was in tears while my mom was trying to calm her, offering her tissues and hot tea. Mom glanced over at me and I could see the alarm on her face that I had overheard Jackie's news. This news meant CJ's dad wouldn't be around for CJ's birthday tomorrow either. Mom offered for our family to take CJ out for his birthday to go get Pizza and see a movie, but Jackie said CJ didn't want to do anything. She said he was having a really hard time making friends. He's just so insecure about his dyslexia. He's upset about the impending divorce. At that, Mom gave me a look that said, "Go away now or you will never celebrate Christmas again."

Even though we were only talking on the phone, I could tell Joel was jumping up and down with the information he had discovered. I tried to calm him down. "Look, Uhmm, my mom has become friends with his mom and actually they were over here today. Things are not so good in his family and I think that's why he's been so horrible to Dirk and others at school. It's not good and it's not what you're thinking."

"What is it then? What's going on with the biggest faker on the planet?" Joel was still angry. "I knew he wasn't a normal sixth-grader."

"I will tell you, if only you promise not to tell a soul. Got it?"

"Yeah, sure. But he's still a faker and I now know the truth. That's all that matters," Joel said.

"Joel, you can't repeat any of this," I begged. "I am serious."

"Fine. I won't tell Mandy or Piper then," Joel huffed.

"O.k. that's a start," I said.

"Tell me now," Joel demanded. "What do you know about the world's worst sixth-grader?"

"His parents are getting divorced. Mom said that's probably why he's been "so unsettled" at school, as she calls it; why he's been acting out, being a bully, telling weird stories, at least that's what my mom thinks. He's having a hard time adjusting to his new life without his dad around."

"Oh." Joel whispered.

Joel and Artie didn't have anything else to say. At that moment, I realized how petty I was about not wanting CJ to eat my mom's pies, and how I thought today was my worst Christmas ever. The shame I felt made my cheeks hot. I had to go drink several glasses of water to cool down. It was if I was boiling in my own juices.

That night before I went to bed I had a talk with God. I asked God to help CJ. I asked Him to make it possible for CJ and his dad to be together tomorrow on his birthday. Then I thanked God for my family and I really meant it. I wished Jesus a happy birthday and fell asleep.

Chapter Thirty-Two

All the good feelings I had felt toward my family quickly disappeared at about two in the morning. Sam woke up and decided it was the perfect time to play with my new drone. He stood in the living room with the back door open— flying the drone around the backyard. He watched the camera and giggled. When I walked in, he dropped the controls and my drone flew out of our yard and past the neighbor's house.

"Sam!" I whisper-yelled in my most harsh, disapproving older brother voice. "What are you doing? Mom and Dad would be so upset if they knew you were out of bed and playing with the back door open!"

"I'm helping," Sam pointed at the box the drone came in.

"Helping with what?" I really began to wonder about my four-year-old brother.

"I'm looking for monsters and raccoons," Sam pointed at the back yard.

"No, you're playing. There's nothing to fear out there. You know that. This is all going to blow over very soon." I looked out the backdoor, "Where's the drone?"

Sam shrugged. I grabbed the camera and saw that the drone was at the edge of our neighborhood. It soared toward the downtown area of Cedarville.

"Uh, oh…." I stepped outside and looked across the sky. The drone dropped in altitude. It looked like it could be crashing soon. "Stay there and don't touch the controller. I'll be right back." Without any other thought of how I could explain that the drone had suddenly disappeared in the night, I jumped after it." The night air was cold, and my feet were colder. Each time I landed, my toes felt like they were frozen in ice cubes. The cold air made it hard for me to jump and so instead of jumping over nine houses at a time, I could only jump eight, then seven, then six, then…five. The colder I became—the less I could move. I didn't bring a jacket, I was wearing my pajamas without shoes.

After following it through my neighborhood, I saw it crash into the front yard of a home on the edge of a neighboring subdivision. The drone had wedged itself into the upper branches of an old oak tree. While jumping up to retrieve it, I broke several small branches. Luckily the drone was in good shape. I looked around quickly to make sure no one saw me. Every house was dark against the night sky, including the one I stood in front of.

I made my way home but could only jump three houses at a time. Every time I pushed off the roofs or chimneys of houses I felt a horrible sting of cold like knives in my feet. After I got home, I realized Sam had waited up for me. I limped in through the backdoor, put the drone on the couch and hauled Sam over my shoulder back to bed. I "shushed" him to stop him from giggling when I heard Libby's bedroom door open. She was headed into the bathroom. I froze where I was standing until Libby shut the bathroom door. Then, for the first time in forever, I jumped down the hallway and landed in front of Sam's bedroom door. I quietly tucked him into bed while he still tried not to giggle. I waited in his room until Libby had gone back to sleep then tiptoed back to my room.

I woke up at eight the next morning as Mom stood in my doorway, wanting to know if I had unlocked the back door. Panic rose up in me like a really bad burrito and I thought I might throw up. How had I forgotten to lock the back door? I acted super sleepy and told her that I thought all doors were locked. This is actually true. I mean, I did think I had locked the door. She then went to Libby's room while

I went straight to Sam's room and told him not to tell Mom and Dad about our adventure last night.

Four year-olds are not very good at keeping a plan together. At breakfast, Sam giggled as I made a face about our breakfast of buckwheat porridge. I couldn't help it. Mom thought she was awesome when she topped our bowls off with a spoonful of plain yogurt mixed with pureed yellow squash. She was so quick that I didn't have time to yank my bowl away from her. I'm sorry but there is no amount of nutmeg and cinnamon that's going to make this taste good. Thus, I blame squash for the complete mess my life has become.

When Sam giggled about my gross breakfast topping, it gave Libby a flicker of memory from last night. "What a minute!?!" She looked at Sam, then me, back to Sam and gave me the most ruthless side-eye as she hollered, "Mom! Mom! Sam and Alex were up goofing around last night when I went to the bathroom. I bet they left the back door unlocked!! They did it! I am positive!"

"What?!?" Mom stood over me, "What did you do?! Why weren't you in bed?! Why did you leave the house unlocked so that something very bad could happen to you?!! Why, Alex why?!!" My mom finally caught her breath.

"Uhmm, so I woke up and found Sam playing in the living room with my new drone and he had opened the back door to check for monsters. I had a talk with Sam last night…. Right, Sam? He promised to never do it again and then I thought I locked the door. I really did. Then I put Sam to bed, and I went to sleep too. That's what happened."

Mom lunged toward my brother. "Sam, my poor dear Sam, nothing is going to happen to us. Your father and I won't let anything bad happen to you." She picked up Sam in her arms and held him, brushing back his hair with her hand. I think Mom was relieved that Sam actually showed some normal level of fear or at least concern about what is happening around town. However, Sam went back to giggling as Mom tried her best to soothe and comfort a child who was anything but scared. Mom was so worked up, she didn't even notice his laughter. But Libby looked suspiciously at me, with her cold, steely eyeballs. Dad looked at me and Libby with absolute confusion.

It only took thirty more minutes and a phone call before Mom was on the couch clutching a pillow and golf club, while straining to tell us, "Everything is fine. Just fine. Absolutely fine. Nothing to worry about. Alex, where's your flashlight? Libby, why don't you bring me you're really big cheerleading trophy, you know, the big one, that's heavy. Bring me that one so we can look at it. Sam, you stay here next to me, right next to me."

Clearly something was wrong with Mom. Dad returned to the living room to inform all of us that all windows and doors were locked. He also stated that Jackie would keep us updated and that we were to watch the noon news.

With a pile of baseball bats, golf clubs, and Libby's trophy set in the middle of the living room as our stockpile of weapons—our family gathered together to watch the noon news. At 12:01 Kelly Meadows reported live on the air, standing in Mr. Hughes front yard. This was the same Mr. Hughes whose cat, Oliver, went missing for a week.

"Well, I came out around 8:15 this morning after Oliver and I ate breakfast," Mr. Hughes began.

"So, you found your cat then?" Kelly Meadows asked. "Do you think Frogman had anything to do with your cat's disappearance. Did you suspect your cat was kidnapped? Was there a ransom? Did you pay?"

"Well, I..." Mr. Hughes spoke sheepishly into the microphone. "I got a phone call from an animal rescue shelter. He had been picked up and transferred to a shelter across the county due to overcrowding. We were reunited the next morning when staff recognized Oliver's picture on television." The camera panned over to the front window of Mr. Hughes home where Oliver, sprawled on the sill, watched the commotion in the front yard. He gave a ginormous yawn and the camera cut back to Kelly Meadows.

"Tell me what you discovered this morning in your own front yard, under this very tree," Kelly Meadows pointed to an oak tree behind her. There in the background Joel worked with two officers from the State Police.

"Oliver and I had just had breakfast when I came out to get the paper. Oliver loves to read the funnies right after breakfast. We always read the funnies first, then it's the crossword puzzle. The Gazette had been tossed under the tree and when I went to get it, I noticed I had some broken branches lying under the tree," Mr. Hughes pointed to the branches lying on the ground. "It was strange because we didn't have strong winds last night. As I leaned over to pick it up, I saw some very unusual foot prints by the branches on the ground. That's when I called the police and Joel Hutchins. It's very unsettling."

"You heard it here first." Kelly Meadows said as the camera cut to footage of my footprints under Mr. Hughes tree. "Frogman is on the loose in the Oak Creek neighborhood. He is breaking tree branches and reading the Cedarville Gazette. This is Kelly Meadows reporting. Back to you in studio."

Mom shut off the television and went to the den to talk with Dad for the next two hours. Joel's website had 32,000 more hits by 1 p.m. By that evening he had gained over another 80,000 followers. By morning, Saturday the 27th, Joel was back on top of the world. He was busy making new videos for his website. One of which was an interview with Mandy who gave her thoughts on "Frogman." She shared what she thought Piper thought of "Frogman." Since he got to spend time with Mandy today, Joel seemed to be backing off of the whole CJ ordeal. But my nightmare was just beginning.

Chapter Thirty-Three

I finished breakfast when the doorbell rang. Mom practically ran to the door and in walked a woman with a blue jacket and black pants. She had a tablet with her and Mom eagerly took her on a tour of our house. After forty minutes, she left. Mom didn't say a word to us about who the strange woman was, but there really wasn't time to talk. Our phone continued to ring all morning and into the afternoon until it was time for another Monster Club meeting. At this session, Mom announced that all new meetings would be run by Mr. Gerald Pyke. The meetings would also move to his residence—one street over. Then she served coffee and cake. I should have known that something was terribly wrong, but I was too distracted by Mr. Brandt's all-day basketball clinic.

Sunday morning, as we pulled out of our garage to go to church, I discovered in our yard the most frightening and alarming thing I had ever seen.

"Oh, gosh. Just a second kids. That's not supposed to be there." Mom was already trying to calm us all down.

Libby began to cry and tried to push back her tears. Sam, of course was fine because he can't read. He is so lucky! I tried to slow my breathing and not jump through the window, across the yard, down the street, and to my favorite place in the world, that muddy pond.

"Hold up! There's been a misunderstanding," Dad chimed in. "That wasn't supposed to be there until tomorrow. It's all going to be alright. Everything is fine."

It wasn't fine. My mom was so freaked out about "Frogman," who is really me, that she convinced my dad to move—Far, far away to a distant land unknown to monsters with froggy feet, Chuparaccoons, and coyotes that eat boxes of pancake mix on aisle nine at Graysons Grocery.

Needless to say, I didn't know who was having a worse day—Me, Libby, or CJ. We went to church and sang Christmas carols but looked like we were at a funeral. Nate, our youth pastor, asked what was wrong but none of us felt liked talking.

For the rest of the day, we cleaned our house, top to bottom. It was horrible. Then on Monday, the tours of our house began. Total strangers came through to take my home away from me. This was when Sam really began to understand what was happening. He stayed with me in my room the entire morning crying. I had to do something. I took Sam and went to Artie's to discuss a plan.

And the plan was I need to come clean.

But how? How do you tell your parents, the school, the town, and the State Police, that you are the Boogeyman that they are so afraid of? Would I be arrested? Would I go to prison? Would they believe me about that crazy looking frog at the beach? Would Joel analyze me every day in a huge petri dish, write best-selling books about me, and ensure that I will never have a date? Would Joel forgive me that I told Artie I was "Frogman" but didn't tell him? Would I be a better friend to Joel? Would they always accuse me of eating cats and dogs when someone's pet goes missing? Would my mom be upset that I like to eat bugs? Would my mom always be afraid of me? Will she try to run away from the one thing she can't run away from which is...me? Could I continue to be "me" even if everyone else thinks I am a monster?

"Hey! Come on! Let's try to figure out a plan." Artie clapped his hands in front of my face, bringing me back to our conversation. "I think you might be running out of options. I realize you tried to lay low but things happen. They'll happen again. You can't be sure they won't. Maybe everyone will be understanding. Maybe they won't arrest you. Maybe they will see that you were only trying to help." Artie sat on his bed, his fingers wiggling and trembling at super-sonic speed.

"I have to do something. Every crazy thing in town that's happening now, is because of me. The food traps: pizza and hotdogs dangling from trees as if there were pinecones; that's because of me. The growing population of coyotes that are now running through our streets and stores; that's because of me. Raccoons hanging out in front of Bob's Burger Barn begging for french fries; that's because of me. The poop that is splattered all over our yards, parking lots, and sidewalks; that's because of me. Well, not me, exactly...but you know, what I mean."

"Well, yeah..." Artie shook his head in agreement. He looked somewhat sad. "You know, if we hadn't gone to Dirk's Halloween party, none of this would have ever happened. But, who's to say if Dirk and Piper would have been rescued? I know people think you're a monster. I know that you've been wondering that too. But you're not. Whatever happens and no matter how many bugs you eat, you still saved Dirk and Piper. They are here because of you. You're a hero."

"Thanks Artie," I said.

It was good to hear my best friend tell me that he didn't think I was a monster. I finally believed it myself. I trusted God wasn't pulling some crazy prank

278

on me, and that I now craved beetles and spiders because He wanted me to be weird. God had a plan for all of this, but maybe it was time to reveal what I thought was His plan.

For the next several mornings I considered telling my parents the truth about the frog on the beach, and my funky new feet. Coming clean with the truth was the only option I saw that would keep us from moving. Every time I tried to broach the subject about "Frogman" Mom tried to reassure me how the police and military were going to catch this animal and put him away for good. She would remind me not to fear because once this horrible beast was caught everything would return to normal. "Let's not worry ourselves over it. We don't need to talk about it. Only happy thoughts!" She'd say with a smile and then tell us to make sure our rooms were clean because potential home buyers were coming over to look at the house.

My mom constantly looked out our windows, peered up and down our street, and flew the drone around the neighborhood. Not only was she looking for the star in the morning, now after dinner she would drive around our town searching for it until dark. Only one picture had been in the news since December 22. She was sure the star would have been returned by Christmas and had asked the police department to set up cameras to catch the culprit in the act of returning the star. But the star never returned. There were no suspects. All anyone knew was that star was gone. And with two strange occurrences in our town, Mom naturally put together that "Frogman" had swiped the star.

During this time, Joel started his own ViewTube channel and had hundreds of thousands of views. He made a video every day with the new camera he got for Christmas. He even interviewed Piper's mom for one segment. In a second segment, he interviewed Artie as another eyewitness to the "Frogman" sighting at the Marshall House. This interview lasted thirty seconds. Artie looked as if he would pass out. Artie just said over and over again, "I don't know what I saw. It was so dark and I had smoke in my eyes. That's what I remember. It was dark and I really didn't see much." Even in an interview in which Artie gave so little information, he had 168,243 views.

With my new footprints discovered under Mr. Hughes tree, Soren Bergman was once more interested in coming to Cedarville with his production crew from Beast T.V. to interview Joel for his television show. Soren made it absolutely clear to Joel that he believed he was telling the truth and considered his photographs to be untouched and authentic. But just as Soren apologized for doubting Joel's prior claims about "Frogman" and for any misunderstanding that Joel 'hoaxed' the photographs and prints, Joel did something so unexpected, even his parents were caught off guard. Joel turned down Soren and his offer to be on his television program. A television show, as Joel boasted, that is seen by millions and millions of viewers. I was stunned. Artie was stunned. Wasn't this the very thing Joel wanted all along—to be proven truthful and honest? Didn't he want his pen pals to know, as well as millions of people, that he was not a "hoaxer?"

"Look, here's the deal..." Joel began as Artie and I stood stunned in Joel's living room. "If Soren wants me to come on his show so badly now and when I have accumulated a lot, I MEAN A LOT, of subscribers and viewers to my ViewTube channel, website, and Facelook page, why in the world would I do it now? Why would I do his show when I can do my own internet show right here from Cedarville with you two, my very best buds helping me to solve cases of the weird, strange, and amphibian? I am going to do my own show called, 'Investigating Investigations about Investigations.' It's going to be fantastic. We're going to be famous. We're going to be rich. We'll get to camp in the woods all the time and go on night explorations." Joel was off in la la land.

Artie's fingers twitched again, he leaned over and whispered, "Is this for real? Are we really going to be internationally known as monster hunters and spend our days trying to ignore the fact that you're Frogman? I had been thinking about becoming a competitive bowler. You know, go to college on a bowling scholarship, and then open my own chain of bowling alleys."

"He's just super excited, I think. Maybe he'll calm down in a few days. Maybe he'll go back to researching CJ and maybe things will die down," I said trying to believe that things would get better.

Joel finished his lengthy discourse on his future and said he needed to get back to work. He planned to tape an interview with the whole Glitterati, excluding Piper, today. He needed time to prepare before the taped interview. I was curious about this interview but he told us that we wouldn't be needed today as he already wrote up his questions.

Later, Artie and I discussed how things would change when I came clean about my true identity. I tried to find a way to tell my parents, but it never seemed like a good time. It was chaos between all of the house showings, Mom's search for the star, and sorting through our clothes and Sam's toys before we packed up the house to move.

I finally decided that New Year's day would be the day I would tell my parents about the new, real, me. I would start the new year without any secrets, and live fully as my true self. No more hiding my funky feet or my appetite for worms and crickets. I would tell them after breakfast, after they had their coffee. Hopefully they would understand that we don't have to move. We don't have to sell the only home I have ever known and move far away from Artie and Joel and Piper. Why, God, why did this happen to my feet and my life? Please help!

Chapter Thirty-Four

New Year's Eve morning, the real estate agent called my dad to let him know there was a buyer interested in our home. This news sent my mom into a fit of celebratory laughter and sudden pangs of sadness. She was happy to move so her family would be safe, but like me, she was somber about moving away from the only home her children had known. Later that afternoon, Jackie called. She invited Mom and Dad out to a New Year's Eve party, which was also a "going away party" our neighbors and friends put together. Many people in the community wanted to thank my mom for all she had done for the Historical Society.

Mom was in such a terrific mood that she allowed Artie and Joel to spend the night and rented movies and video games. She even brought home seven large pizzas with chips, candy, and soda! This would be the best New Year's Eve ever! Libby, Sam and I danced around the pile of junk food. We couldn't believe our luck. There was so much "garbage" food, as Mom calls it, we couldn't imagine eating all of it in one night.

The doorbell rang and Mom practically floated to the door. She was in such a good mood. But that's when the entirety of her hideous plot became known. There in the doorway, looking upset and agitated, were Katie, CJ, and Ryker. Mom hustled them inside, showed them the movies we were to watch and then announced that Ryker was in charge. She said that she, Dad, and Jackie were going to pop over to the Wilson's to celebrate for a bit. "After all, wouldn't it be nice for all of us to celebrate the new year together?" She gave Ryker her cell phone number and whispered to Libby to keep an eye on all of us, including Ryker since he probably hadn't babysat much.

Normally, Libby would have been angry at the thought that she needed to be supervised, but since it was Ryker, she acted like it was some kind of parental appointed date. She made googly eyes at him and laughed at his every word.

"So, what kind of pizza did your mom get?" Ryker asked Libby.

"Uh, huhhhhhhhhhhh...." Libby giggled and fluttered her eyes as if gnats just landed on her eyelashes.

"So…..?" Ryker looked annoyed.

"I don't know. Let's find out." Libby hip-checked Joel and pushed Artie away from the table.

"Ryker flipped each box open and stood over the pizzas taking first pick. Libby smacked Joel's hand as he tried to reach around for a slice of pizza. "So rude! Guests first!" Libby smiled at Ryker but he never looked up.

"I'm a guest." Joel stammered.

"Yeah, no," Libby countered, still smiling at Ryker who now left the table to sit on the sofa. At the same time, I felt bad for Artie as he sulked over a bowl of chips and watched Libby try to act cool around Ryker.

With Ryker out of the way, we gathered around the dining table and went after the pizza. Joel, of course, couldn't help himself when it came to annoying CJ. Every time CJ went to grab a slice of pizza, Joel reached in and grabbed it first. Joel did it three times until I pulled him away from the table.

"That's enough for you!" I lowered my voice to a whisper and spoke slowly so Joel would not misunderstand. "Remember what I told you. CJ had a horrible Christmas and birthday. Tis the season to forgive and forget. Be nice."

Joel agreed that it would be hard for him to go through what CJ had experienced and swore on his honor to try to get along. CJ's plate was overloaded with pizza but I was relieved that CJ hadn't sneezed, wheezed or coughed all over our dinner.

Joel, Artie, and I set up camp in front of the television to play video games. Artie kept looking over his shoulder to watch then sulk every time Libby smiled in Ryker's direction. CJ slowly made his way over toward us and ate silently from the couch as he watched us rifle through our pile of video games. That's when Ryker spoke up.

"Ok. In order for things to go smoothly tonight. I will need you all to do several things. First, eat your dinner, then clean up after yourself, and the oldest gets to choose which video games and movies we watch tonight. In case there is any confusion... that would be me." Ryker doubled thumbed himself to reiterate his point. He grabbed up his backpack and rifled through it.

Joel and Artie gave me a look as if I invited them to a manicure and pedicure party. I looked at Libby, who shrugged her shoulders. Sam immediately said he wanted to watch his favorite cartoon. Katie flopped on the floor of the living room and said she didn't want to watch babyish movies. She wanted to watch the fireworks at the park for New Year's Eve. That's when Sam started wailing.

"I want to watch fireworks and my movie," Sam hollered through his tears.

"We can watch the fireworks later tonight through the windows, because your mom said we aren't allowed to go outside. I left a few of my things back at home. I'm going to go get them and come right back. Sam, you can watch your movie until I come back. Lock the doors and don't do anything stupid while I'm gone."

Just like that, Ryker walked out the front door and disappeared.

Chapter Thirty-Five

"Okay, okay. I'm in charge while he's gone. Sam you can watch your movie in Mom and Dad's room. Grab a blanket and get on their bed. I will be right there to turn the television on for you. Guys do your thing over there, away from me," Libby pointed to the living room, "Got it. And keep it down." Libby followed after Sam.

We each grabbed a video game controller, including CJ, and immediately were involved in a ninja conspiracy to take down the bad guys. Joel actually was being cool about CJ playing with us but Katie got bored and whiny.

"Look in Ryker's backpack and see if he brought his tablet. You can play on that," CJ tried to fight back against Joel's army of ninjas.

Katie dug into Ryker's backpack and pulled out his tablet. Libby, who had returned from taking care of Sam, was now interested in Ryker's tablet. Katie typed in a password and started swiping while Libby watched closely next to her.

"It won't open." Katie fumed.

"I'm a little busy. Alex, can you help Katie." CJ said as he battled against Joel and his squad of warriors.

I went over to Katie as she held the tablet out to me. I grabbed it and flopped on the couch next to her and started to open up programming files searching for the game she wanted to play. I clicked on a file. That's when every cell of my body zinged, snapped, and popped. On his tablet was a file titled, "Christmas in Cedarville" with a star next to it.

"Huh...He must really be bored. What's exciting about Christmas in Cedarville? All we have now are monsters." Libby wrinkled her brow then shook her head. She got up and went to the kitchen for a drink. I could tell she was rethinking that Ryker was a cool high schooler.

I, on the other hand, needed Katie's prying eyes off the tablet for two seconds while I opened the file. "Okay, okay... getting a little crowded here. Why don't you get a drink while I fix this for you?"

Katie jumped off the couch in search of more soda. I clicked on the file. Suddenly, I scanned through dozens of photos of the Historical Society's missing star. Every now and then, Ryker would pose with a peace sign in front of the camera lens. Ryker had stolen the Historical Society's star!

While Katie and Libby helped themselves to drinks and chips, I continued to look through the pictures when the phone rang. Yep, you guessed it... Ryker called in to check on us.

"Everything good? Everything under control?" Ryker asked.

"Sure. When are you coming back?" I asked as I heard car tires screech in the back ground while Ryker spoke.

"Soon. I'm still looking for my video game. I think CJ or Katie did something with it. Hey, has my mom called or anything?"

I definitely heard more cars. It sounded like he was outside. "No, why? Is there a problem?"

"Nope, everything's good. Just tried calling her a bit ago. That's all." Ryker's voice sounded somewhat strained.

"So, we will see you soon?" I asked even though I knew he was lying.

"Yep, I'm just a little tied up and then I'll be right back over there!" He hung up. I couldn't wait until he came back. I couldn't wait until Mom and Dad got home and I could bust him. Maybe then my mom would calm down a little bit.

Artie sat inbetween CJ and Joel. Things were not going well as Artie gave me a look over his shoulder that suggested we needed to find something else to do. Joel and CJ were in a heated battle.

"Hey, why don't we watch the movie we rented? It's supposed to be really good," I grabbed up the DVD case and walked toward the TV.

"Yes, let's watch a movie. I'm super bored." Libby grabbed the DVD from my hand, stood in front of the television, and loaded the movie.

Joel and CJ grumbled while Artie approved Libby's decision. While Libby prepped the movie, the news flickered on for a few seconds. Kelly Meadows stood with her microphone in front of our city bridge that crosses our river. It's on the outskirts of town, and emergency vehicles drove behind Kelly as she spoke.

"New Year's prank gone wrong? We won't know for certain until this person is rescued from the top of Cedarville's River Street bridge. And to add to the mystery, it looks like the missing star is strapped to the bridge too." Kelly Meadows beamed with uncontrollable excitement.

Dangling from the bridge 100 feet above the river, dressed in jeans and a dark jacket was Ryker. I recognized Ryker immediately, but CJ and Katie had not, which was probably best. It appeared, as the camera zoomed in, that Ryker was tangled in bungee cords that held him to the bridge. Right above him was the Star, strapped onto the bridge with more bungee cords. In an instant, Ryker dropped two feet. The cords were stretching loose. As I looked at the television, I saw they were trying to get boats into place. They had several firetrucks on the bridge but none of their ladders were tall enough to reach him."

"Whoa! That doesn't look like an overgrown frog to me. That looks like a person, some stupid guy," Libby shook her head. "What an idiot!"

"No, that's not Frogman. I don't know who that guy is. What a weirdo! Doesn't he know that weather report was calling for sleet and ice tonight? That bridge is probably frozen over already." Joel tossed his controller to the side.

Artie looked at me and his hands began to quiver. He already knew what I was thinking.

"I am not feeling too good, Libby. I think all of that real pizza and soda is making me sick. Maybe Mom knows what she is talking about." I ran off into the direction of Mom and Dad's room and locked myself in their bathroom. Artie was right behind me.

Through the door, I quickly told Artie my plan. "Go to my room and get my black hoodie and gloves. They're in the closet, and grab my black basketball shoes." Artie ran off to my room, with Sam on his heels. Sam helped him gather what I asked for. I opened the bathroom door, grabbed the clothes and told them both to tell Libby that I was sick to my stomach. I told them to say I was camping out in Mom and Dad's bathroom and would give updates on my condition every ten minutes until I returned.

"What are you going to do?" Artie asked, unsure if he really wanted to know.

"That's Ryker. He needs help and if I can get that star back to Mom and her Historical Society then maybe we won't have to move. But first, Ryker is in real danger. It's easy to see he won't be able to hold it together for much longer. So far, no one has been able to reach him. Listen, for now, you can't tell anyone it's him. Got it?"

"Right, okay, got it." Artie said.

"Got it." Sam repeated.

I shut the bathroom door and locked it. Then I opened the bathroom window, climbed out, and jumped over houses, until I came to the river. It didn't take long and now more boats headed to the bridge. I could see Ryker dangling from the side of the bridge. I could hear him yelling too. He was screaming for help.

294

All at once, he dropped another foot as the people below gasped. He quieted too, but only for a moment. Then he was screaming for help again. I stretched my hoodie over my head and creeped to the bank of the river. The leaves crunched under my weight. I could see ice forming across the leaf litter on the ground as the sleet blew in my face. Police Chief Carlton attempted to climb up the side of the bridge pulling himself up a third of the way before getting stuck. I could only imagine how slippery and icy the bridge had become. The Fire Chief stood atop the fire truck ladder but was still a good fifteen feet too short of reaching Ryker.

I took a few more steps toward the river, reached down and smeared mud all over my jeans, hoodie, face, hands, and hair, when eye shine caught my attention. It was, in fact, three pairs of yellowish eyes glowing in the dark. I stepped closer and there huddled under a tree were three raccoons downing a plate of tacos.

Fish tacos to be exact, with a side of mango salsa, tortilla chips, and a huge splat of guacamole. It was obvious that the raccoons were not fans of the avocado. While they completely ignored the boats, the police cars, and the fire engines, they sniffed the air in my direction, and one by one they dropped their chips and tacos, and sat up on their back haunches—smiling at me.

Chapter Thirty-Six

It was then I realized they were not expressing friendliness, but were actually flashing their jagged little teeth at me. Somehow, they knew or smelled that I was froggish. It was like they could see right through my tennis shoes and now they had the perfect side dish to those fish tacos; frog legs. I couldn't move. I froze in fear while my insides began to freeze. In my hurry, I forgot to bring a jacket. My legs felt like two-ton blocks of ice. I realized now, that in the cold I couldn't stop moving or I would risk freezing in place. Those horrible masked mammals stepped closer to me and separated. Two flanked my right and left side, while the biggest one slowly crept towards me, his eyes glowing, his teeth gnashing together. He opened his mouth wide and reached out his two tiny, yet frightening, little hands towards my feet. In one jump, he was attached to my leg. I would have been worried that they were rabid but then I remembered that frogs can't get rabies...

Suddenly, Ryker's plight didn't seem so important anymore. All I could think was, "Raccoons eat frogs! Raccoons eat frogs! And I am surrounded!" This was how it was all going to end; me on a paper plate squished inside a flour tortilla! "God please help MEEEEE!"

And in that moment, God heard me. How do I know? Because the crowd of spectators, reporters, and emergency operators gasped in unison, as Ryker slipped another foot. But I also heard a shrill shriek I had come to know well in my twelve years on this planet. Mostly when an uninvited spider ambushed her in the shower, or when she woke up in the morning and realized she was out of coffee. It was my mom.

She was there in the crowd and she screamed because the star was also slipping out of the bungee cords that held it to the bridge. I'm positive she was very anxious about Ryker as well. That chorus of gasps distracted those evil raccoons, including the one that was now on my back and clinging to my left shoulder. I could feel it's breath on my neck when my mom's scream distracted it, as well as the one now clinging to my left foot and the other that was inches from my right leg. They turned toward my mom's ear-piercing scream just long enough for me to will myself to jump to the side of the river. Two boats below the bridge held spotlights on Ryker as he slipped through the cords, still hollering for help. He was now holding onto the end of the cord.

I kicked off my shoes and put them under a tree stump near the tree line. When I moved back to the edge of the river to jump and grab Ryker, I heard blood curdling screams and one splash of water, then another. The bungee cords had given way, sending Ryker and the wooden star to the freezing watery depths below. I didn't expect the star to resurface but I did expect Ryker to. Five seconds, ten seconds… The boats shined their lights into the dark, cold waters but there was no sign of Ryker. I knew the icy waters would slow me down, and maybe freeze me like a frog popsicle until spring, but it was a risk I had to take. I had to try to save Ryker. As I leapt through the air, I realized I had company. That ravenous raccoon was still attached to my back and while we were in mid-air he panicked, climbing onto my shoulder and pulling my hoodie over my eyes. I couldn't see a thing and said another quick prayer for my aim to be true.

In a half second we splashed through the river's surface. The cold water shocked my system as if I had plunged through a frozen wall of ice while glacial shards skewered my body. I panicked when I realized I couldn't move. My hands and feet, were weighted down as if my muscles had turned to stone. I sank under the waves, into the dark waters, where the spotlights overhead couldn't shine. I felt myself slowly begin to settle in for the rest of the winter, sinking toward the bottom of the river. I struggled to keep my eyes open, as the most powerful urge to sleep overtook my senses. I remembered thinking about Mom and Dad. Would they worry what had become of me? I also wondered if I would awaken in the spring thaw, and if I would be allowed to finish sixth grade? I also remembered thinking about Ryker and if he were sleepy too? I saw him... just a fleeting glance. He was well below me. I closed my eyes and went to sleep.

Chapter Thirty-Seven

I couldn't have been in hibernation mode but for a second or two when my nerves rattled my brain back awake. It was the raccoon. It's left hand dug into my left ear, its other hand ripped at my hair, while one of its feet tangled inside my hoodie. The claws on its other back foot scratched at my back as it desperately tried to free itself and swim to the surface.

In a flash, I was wide awake, in awful pain, but remembered why I was sinking to the bottom of the river. I could still see Ryker. He had nearly reached the bottom. I needed help as I still felt like cement filled my muscles and ran through my veins. I said another quick prayer and as if on cue that raccoon yanked my hair so hard, I kicked my legs. The raccoon pulled my hair again and now I was kicking my legs and cutting through the water. I was within reach of Ryker in another second. I wrapped my arms underneath his and locked my hands in front of his chest.

It seemed the raccoon was really freaking out about adding a third to our little swim party as it sunk its teeth into my scalp. If only he could understand why I had to do what I was about to do. With Ryker in place, I said another quick prayer for help, and actually kicked as hard as I could deeper into the black waters below. It was only another second or two, and I know it was the wrong direction, and I know Ryker and the raccoon were nearly drowned, but I needed to hit the bottom. HARD! Super HARD! Finally reaching the bottom of the river I gave the biggest push of my life! It was the only way to get the lift to reach the other side of the river.

The three of us breached the surface of the river and flew through the air, the men working the two search lights on the boats struggled to follow us as we landed in the woods on the far side of the river. The air was electric with screams and shouts. I saw two police cars and an ambulance backing up in reverse on the bridge in an effort to find us.

The raccoon jumped off my head and disappeared into the brush. I could still hear it hissing at me as it scurried away. But, Ryker wasn't moving. Even his eyes didn't open when I poked him with a stick. I began to fear the worst, when suddenly he gasped, coughed, sucked in a whole lot of air and puked all over everything!

It was disgusting. While he threw up, I smeared vomit-less mud all over my face, hoodie, jeans, and feet, and stood behind a tree. When Ryker rolled over and saw me, he just started screaming. Like a girl. Like Katie, in fact.

That was my cue to leave…like fast…like NOW! I was still super cold, and my muscles felt sluggish but my adrenaline told me otherwise. But before I could go home there was just one more thing that had to be done. I had to save the star. Maybe Mom would change her mind about moving if I could get it back. Maybe I wouldn't have to say goodbye to Artie, Joel, and of course, Piper. Maybe someone, somewhere, would realize I am not the monster they think I am. Maybe Ryker would be able to tell the truth about me, that he's in the woods barfing because of me. Wait? WHAT? YOU know what I mean…

I jumped up and over into the middle of the river to the sound of more shouts, more screams, and now to the sound of the Cedarville's New Year's Eve fireworks display booming, and popping in our local park. I was cold and groggy, super groggy, as I dove back into the water. I kicked toward the star that was lodged upright on the bottom of the river bed. I grabbed it and pushed back the overwhelming desire to sleep. Instead, I kicked off the bottom of the river once again. Luckily, the lights on the boats were unable to track me as I landed near my shoes. I quickly put them on, said goodbye to the two raccoons, and headed home. That is, not before leaving the star out of the reach of any type of surveillance camera, but where someone would find it: I dropped it off at

Heartwood stables; inside a barn, leaning against a feeding trough. It seemed to be an obvious place to leave the star; next to a manger.

Back home, I crawled through the window and got into the shower, the warm water brought me back to life as Artie banged on the door.

"I'll be right out!" I yelled.

Artie and Sam had covered for me. A little too well, actually. Artie told the group that eating junk food must have made me sick because after throwing up a few times, I had explosive bowel movements all over my clothes and was in the shower trying to get clean. CJ cackled with laughter at my demise. Joel was repulsed and covered his ears each and every time Artie gave an update on my condition. Because Libby was beyond grossed out by Artie's details, she never checked up on me.

I got out of the shower, dressed and joined the others just in time for my parents to come home. Mom and Dad took CJ and Katie into the kitchen for a private conversation. Of course, I listened in. Mom and Dad told them about Ryker, that he was safe, but that he was at the hospital with their mom, just to make sure all was well. Katie looked upset, but CJ looked annoyed, a bit angry, but said nothing. Then they returned to the living room and Mom flipped on the news. Kelly Meadows replayed Ryker and the star falling into the water, over and over again. She slowed the tape down and three times in a row, she pointed to me, a dark dash of a blob, diving into the water, then jumping out with Ryker and disappearing on the far side of the river's bank. The camera then swished, turned, and blurred around when I jumped back in the river to get the star. Kelly Meadows turned to interview Police Chief Carlton on camera.

"Is this the return of Frogman? Does he have a partner? Did he just save that teenager from a very real tragedy?"

"No comment. There's much work to be done. We are elated that the youth in question is safe. Thank you." Police Chief Carlton turned and walked away. The camera closed in on Kelly Meadows.

"You heard it here first. This is the first possible Frogman sighting in several months and he may have a partner. We'll keep you updated as more comes in. Back to you in studio."

CJ and Katie spent the night. Jackie stayed with Ryker in the hospital and took him home the next morning. Before I woke up, Jackie came by and picked up CJ and Katie. I was really glad I didn't have to face CJ again. He still snickered about my poopy pants when we went to sleep. Joel didn't care at all about my situation because he was on my computer updating his website about the possible return of Frogman.

When Artie, Joel and I woke up and drug ourselves into the kitchen for breakfast, my dad was reading the front page of the paper.

"Wow! This just gets stranger and stranger. I mean, what is it?" My dad looked at Joel for more commentary.

Joel and Dad looked at the photos together and Dad went to grab a magnifying glass to get a better look.

"Don't you think it's still just a dark blurry blob?" My dad asked Joel.

"That's definitely it. That's Frogman! I knew he'd come back!" Joel was squinting and hovering over the photos.

"It's so crazy. I mean just the weirdest. Who knows what that is?" Artie tried to join in a natural tone of voice.

"I think it needs to rethink its fashion choices. That hat is not working. It's too big. He should just wear a mask." Libby offered, smacking her gum.

"You see a hat in that blurry blob?" Dad asked Libby.

"It does look a bit like a hat or something?" Mom chimed in.

"I like it! It's the greatest hat ever!" Sam chimed in and then jumped on my leg.

I reached up and touched my hair. I actually could use a hat right now. My scalp was sore from all that hair pulling by that crazed raccoon. I probably had some bald patches.

While the rest of Cedarville contemplated my fashion choices, Mom got a call around ten and ran to the police station. The star had been found. It was all over the news for several days. There was no doubt that I, Frogman, had rescued Ryker and the missing star. And now with Joel as one of my greatest supporters and defenders, Police Chief Carlton, along with our mayor had halted their hunt and sent away the State Police and Texas Rangers. Traps were recovered at the Chief's request and food was no longer to be set out as bait. Chief Carlton in an interview three days later admitted that maybe "Frogman" wasn't dangerous and was instead misunderstood. He suggested that maybe we got it all wrong on Halloween—that it had no ill intent toward our community. What if Frogman showed up to save those kids?"

Now that "Frogman" was possibly no longer a monster, and was getting positive press in the paper, on the nightly news, and over social media, Mom had a change of heart. She knew there was no denying that "Frogman" recovered the missing star from the bottom of the river. A few days later, she walked out into the yard and yanked up the "For Sale" sign and threw it in the trash bin. God had heard my prayers. We were staying. But it was a mixed blessing. To deflect attention that his brother had stolen the star, CJ told everyone about New Year's Eve; specifically, that while fireworks were going off over Cedarville City Park, my colon exploded.

CJ told everyone how I rang in the new year locked in the bathroom for over an hour while I cleaned crap from all my nooks and crannies. At this point in the day at school, I wished we were moving. Especially when I peered out the window during seventh period. I tell you, this is the absolute truth, that there, with its freaky little fingers pressed against the glass, and chewing a piece of bubble gum was that raccoon. It had found me. And I'm not lying one bit when I tell you that there, in its creepy little hand, was a clump of my hair. So, that is how I came to have scratches on my shoulders and bald spots on my scalp.

Do you believe me now?

About E.R. Cosentino

Emily Cosentino was born in Austin, Texas and attended Texas Tech University studying Radio and Television Broadcasting. She received her M.A. in Film Production from Regent University. She kicked around Los Angeles working various jobs in television and film. She now lives in Pennsylvania with her husband and three young children. She's a champion of misfits and late bloomers, and she's addicted to office supplies.

For more information about Emily Cosentino, please visit:

www.EmilyCosentino.com

Made in the USA
Coppell, TX
06 May 2020

24195741R00174